Hershell Cobwell and the Miraculous Tattoo

Other Avon Camelot Books by
George Edward Stanley

THE CODEBREAKER KIDS
THE CODEBREAKER KIDS RETURN
THE ITALIAN SPAGHETTI MYSTERY
THE UKRAINIAN EGG MYSTERY

GEORGE EDWARD STANLEY is a professor of Spanish, Italian, and Romanian at Cameron University and is a past member of the Board of Directors of the Society of Children's Book Writers. Dr. Stanley now lives in Lawton, Oklahoma, with his wife and two sons.

Hershell Cobwell and the Miraculous Tattoo

George Edward Stanley

HERSHELL COBWELL AND THE MIRACULOUS TATTOO is an original publication of Avon Books. This work has never before appeared in book form.

AVON BOOKS
A division of
The Hearst Corporation
105 Madison Avenue
New York, New York 10016

Published by arrangement with the author
Library of Congress Catalog Card Number: 90-93413
ISBN: 0-380-75897-0
RL: 4.8

First Avon Camelot Printing: March 1991

Printed in the U.S.A.

OPM 10 9 8 7 6 5 4 3 2 1

Chapter One

"THERE is absolutely nothing distinctive about you, Hershell Cobwell!" my sister Loretta yelled at me from across the breakfast table. "Absolutely nothing!"

We'd been through this all before, so I did what I always do at breakfast when Loretta's telling me how no-good I am: I read the cereal box.

"Hershell tries, dear," Mom said. She had come into the breakfast room and was buttering herself a piece of toast. "And we must..."

"I know, I know," Loretta said, not even trying to hide the distaste in her voice, "*...be kind to each other.*"

Loretta always finishes Mom's sentences. Actually, Loretta always finishes everybody's sentences.

"Thank you for finishing my sentence, dear," Mom said to her.

Loretta smiled. Coming from Mom, it wasn't a put-down.

Then Loretta looked at me sternly. "It's just that he lacks potential," she added.

I sighed. Loretta was always right, so what she thought about me had to be true, although I'd certainly never admit it to her.

Loretta is very smart. Even though she's just in the eighth grade, she spends her spare time writing term papers that she plans to use when she gets to college.

"Has anybody seen the research papers I was grading last night?" Mom asked.

Mom has a Ph.D. in English, but she's not very good at remembering where she puts things.

"You put them in the oven last night, because it was the only place that wasn't cluttered up with other things," Dad said. He had just come into the room. He took the toast Mom had been buttering and sat down. Dad has a Ph.D. in physics. He looked at me. "Did you do your math problems last night, Hershell?"

"I tried, but I'm not quite sure . . ."

"You should have shown them to me," Loretta interrupted. "I was very good in sixth-grade math. I never made mistakes." She smiled broadly at Mom and Dad, and they smiled back.

"Well, I . . ." I tried to say again.

"I'd have been glad to help you, Hershell," Dad said, "but you have to tell me when you're having trouble."

"I'm always having trouble," I countered. "Besides, you were busy with your computer."

"Oh, well . . ."

"You could have asked me," Mom said, a new piece of toast in her hand.

"But you were reading all those research papers," I said.

"Oh, well . . ."

"Of course, as I indicated a moment ago, I was

available," Loretta declared again. "You could have asked me."

"But I never understand what you're talking about, Loretta," I said.

"Oh, Hershell," Loretta sighed. She turned to Mom and Dad. "I should like very much to help him. It's just that, well, I find it very difficult to come down to his level sometimes." She sighed deeply and went back to eating her toast.

Just once I wish Mom and Dad would realize that Loretta hurts my feelings when she says things like that. But I guess they figure the truth shouldn't hurt anybody's feelings.

"The research papers I was grading last night are not in the oven," Mom declared. "I should like some help in finding them. I have to be at the university in an hour!"

"I'm sure that's where you put them, dear," Dad said.

I realized that I had been dropped as the morning's main topic of discussion, so I said, "Don't worry about me! I'll get by just fine!"

Everyone stopped what he or she was doing and looked at me.

"*Get by!* Hershell, nobody who is anybody just *gets by!*" Dad was finally able to gasp. "I'm sure you didn't intend to say that, son."

"Well, uh, what I meant to say was . . ."

But Mom added quickly, "Yes, Hershell, where would any of us be today, if we just *got by*?"

"Well, uh, it's just that . . ."

"I certainly wouldn't be the most brilliant student at Weatherton Middle School if I just *got by*," Loretta interrupted.

I had to get out of there. "Gee," I said, looking at my watch, "if I don't hurry, I'll be late for school."

"You still have time to finish your breakfast, don't you?" Mom asked. "It's very important that you feed your brain."

"It certainly hasn't seemed to do too much good so far," Loretta said. She sighed deeply again. I was her cross to bear.

I left them all wondering what in the world they could have done wrong to be stuck with someone like me.

I went upstairs and got my books and jacket. If I hurried, I could catch the seven forty-five Broadway bus that went right past Jackson Elementary School, and I wouldn't have to transfer.

Sometimes I wish I went to another school. It's not that I don't like Jackson Elementary, it's just that all my teachers keep comparing me to Loretta. They'll take one look at my papers and say, "Are you *really* Loretta Cobwell's little brother?"

Unlike Loretta, school isn't my whole life. I have varied interests. For instance, I like to collect smashed aluminum cans that look like the faces of people I know.

There are a lot of other things I like to do, too.

But Loretta's right. There is absolutely nothing *distinctive* about me. Actually, I think I'm adopted and that my parents are afraid to tell me in case it might hurt my feelings.

I just sort of blend in.

I am never picked first for any sports team. Sometimes, I'm not picked at all.

I've never been asked to join any clubs or honor societies.

I've never been elected a class officer.

When the school yearbook came out last year, not only did I have nothing listed under my picture, I didn't even have a picture. It simply said, NOT PICTURED: HERSHELL COBWELL. Of course, I suppose I shouldn't complain. Next to my name was another name—NOT PICTURED: JASON LA CHAZZE. At least, they weren't discriminating. I think I'd like to get to know this Jason La Chazze. We probably have a lot in common.

By the time I got to the bus stop, Albuquerque Wilson was already there. Albuquerque lives down the street from me.

"Hi, Albuquerque!" I said.

Albuquerque looked up at me with a puzzled expression on her face. "Do I know you?"

"Sure you do. We've been catching the same bus together for the last five years. I'm Hershell Cobwell."

Albuquerque eyed me carefully, then I saw recognition register. "Are you really Loretta Cobwell's little brother?"

I try not to get angry when people don't remember me, even after the fifth year of our relationship. I have, however, on occasion been known to be sarcastic. "I was last week and I still am," I said with a smile.

Albuquerque didn't smile back.

I really hate to upset people with my biting sarcasm, so I added quickly, "How are Gallup and Tucumcari?"

Mr. and Mrs. Wilson used to live in New Mexico before they moved to San Diego. Gallup and Tucumcari are Albuquerque's younger sisters.

But the bus arrived, and Albuquerque ignored my question. She got on board, took the front seat, and immediately opened her social studies book.

I walked to the back of the bus and took my usual seat, just as the bus lurched away from the curb.

San Diego is a pretty town and I like living here, but when I'm on the bus, I start pretending that I'm going somewhere else to become famous. I always daydream until the bus stops in front of Jackson Elementary School.

"Hey, kid!" the bus driver yelled at me. "Are you going to school today?"

I looked out the window. We were already there. I couldn't believe it. Albuquerque was walking up the steps of the school. But I wasn't ready to get off the bus. I wasn't ready to face anyone yet. I hadn't finished daydreaming.

"Hurry up, kid!" the bus driver shouted again. "I have to get to the foot of Broadway."

I don't know what made me do it, but I said, "That's where I'm going, too. I have to get some information for a report I'm writing."

The driver shrugged his shoulders and pulled away from the curb.

I looked out the window again. Albuquerque and the other kids were going inside the building. Miss Wren would be getting the experiments ready for science class.

I suddenly felt panicky. Why had I told the driver I wanted to go to the foot of Broadway? That was where all the sailors hung out and all the places that the sailors went were. At school, the kids all talked about it.

I remember Allan Binger discussing it once. He was in the sixth grade when I was in the fourth. Allan Binger was always bragging about the movies he had seen in the locker clubs at the foot of Broadway.

I had only been there once and that was with Dad. We had gone to see off an old Admiral friend of his. Of course we hadn't spent any time looking around. Not my dad. Not good old straight-as-an-arrow ex-Navy Commander Clarence Cobwell.

The buildings began to get bigger and taller as we cruised down Broadway. The bus got more crowded, too, and I kept getting short of breath. How was I going to explain all of this? I wondered.

Finally, the driver shouted, "Everybody out!"

I stood up, trying to act as though I knew what I was doing. The driver kept giving me strange looks as I headed toward the door of the bus. I tried not to look at him.

"Hey, kid," he said, as I started down the steps, "are you sure you're supposed to be down here?"

"Of course I'm sure," I said as nonchalantly as I could. "I have an assignment to do."

I started walking the minute I hit the pavement and I didn't stop until I was out of sight of the bus. When I looked up, I was standing in front of the Deep Blue Sea Locker Club.

I had always wondered what a locker club really looked like inside. I never knew how much of what Allan Binger said I could believe. According to him, sailors weren't allowed to keep civilian clothes either on ship or on base, so they rented a locker at a locker club and kept all their civvies there. There were also supposed to be all kinds of other places inside the locker clubs to spend money.

Two guys wearing civilian clothes passed me and went inside. They looked like sailors, so I decided to follow them.

The place was huge. There were stores everywhere. Dry cleaners, jewelry stores, fast-food places, arcades, movies. It was kind of like a seedy mall.

I checked my wallet to see if I had any money. I was surprised to find twenty-five dollars. Then I remembered that ten of it was for lunch this week and ten of it was for the gym equipment use fee that should have been paid two weeks ago. The remaining five was my allowance.

I decided to head for the arcades. I'd worry about eating school lunches and using gym equipment some other time.

There was an attendant standing at the entrance to the arcade.

I handed him ten dollars. "May I have some change, please?"

He gave me a disgusted look, but took my ten dollars anyway. Then he reached into the dirty change apron he had tied around his waist and handed me ten dollars in quarters.

"Thanks," I said. I put the quarters in my pockets. They felt like lead weights.

There weren't too many people in the arcade at this time of the morning. Allan Binger had said that it was really crowded on weekends.

I wandered up and down the aisles until I found a game I wanted to play. It was called Star Monsters. I put a quarter in and pushed the start button.

A couple of sailors came over while I was playing and said something about how good I was. Then they walked on to the next machine. Neither one of them had asked me if I was really Loretta Cobwell's little brother.

I guessed nobody down here had ever heard of Loretta Cobwell. It gave me a feeling of accomplishment to have a couple of sailors think I was good at something. After all, they had seen the world.

After I had spent five dollars on Star Monsters, I began to get bored. Besides, the cigarette smoke was beginning to make me sick.

The attendant looked at me as I was leaving.

"I'll be back," I said. I thought that might change his mind if he was considering reporting me to somebody out of revenge because I hadn't spent all of my ten dollars on his machines.

I wandered around the locker club and looked in several of the stores. There were a lot of people in the fast-food places. How in the world people could keep down chili burgers and chili dogs at this hour of the morning, I had no idea.

I also looked at the pictures advertising the movies that the sailors went to. The only movie I thought might interest me didn't start until one o'clock.

By a clock on the wall, it was eleven. English with Mr. Corvin was just beginning. What were they going to read today? I wondered. I probably wouldn't have liked it anyway. Mr. Corvin was always reading poetry and making up things about what it meant. I could never figure out where he got all of those ideas from the poems he made us read.

I was just about to make up my mind to go back to the arcade when a sign caught my eye: BE DISTINCTIVE! GET A TATTOO! I recalled Loretta's complaint at breakfast that morning: *"There is absolutely nothing distinctive about you, Hershell Cobwell!"*

I walked over to the shop. PAINLESS HARRY'S TATTOO PARLOUR. Another sign read, ARTISTE AT WORK.

The door was open, so I went inside. Harry was busy working on a sailor.

I started looking around. There were all kinds of designs in every imaginable color: yellow flowers, brown and white eagles, pink women, silver knives, and black skulls-and-crossbones.

The sailor suddenly let out a yelp.

"Keep it down," Harry said. "You'll give me a bad reputation."

"Well, it hurts," the sailor whined.

"Of course it does," Harry intoned. "It has to hurt a little. You're getting a tattoo. But when I get through with you, you'll have something you'll be proud of, something you'll take with you to your grave."

"I just hope my girl likes it," the sailor said.

"She'll love it," Harry promised. "I've never known a girl yet who didn't like tattoos."

The sailor smiled.

A few more minutes passed, then Harry said,

"There! It's done! If you have any problems with it, just let me know."

The sailor paid Harry and left, clutching his right arm.

Harry turned to me. "What ship you off of, sailor?"

I've always been tall for my age, but I was surprised by his question. "Uh, uh, we just got in," I managed to mumble.

"Well, what are you looking for?" Harry continued, getting down to business. "A girl? An eagle? How about a nice bouquet of roses with 'MOTHER' written across it?"

"How much does all of this cost?"

"Quality is going to cost you, sailor," Harry hedged, "but you can get a single rose for twelve-fifty. A dozen will cost you twelve times as much."

"Twelve dollars and fifty cents?"

"Okay, okay, for another two and a half, I'll throw in 'MOTHER,'" Harry agreed.

"Fifteen dollars altogether?"

"That's right, and my work is guaranteed," Harry said. "Where do you want it?"

A plan had begun to form in my mind. If it worked, I would be the most distinctive boy at Jackson Elementary School. As far as I knew, nobody else had a tattoo. I, indistinctive Hershell Cobwell, would be distinctive at last!

"Well?" Harry said.

"I'm thinking," I said.

I knew that if I got a tattoo it would have to be on a place where my parents and Loretta wouldn't see it—at least not right away—so that left out my forehead.

Since I wore short-sleeve shirts year round, that left out my arms, too.

Yet it had to be on a part of my body where I could show it off at school without being embarrassed or arrested for indecent exposure. I made my decision and opened my mouth to speak.

"Well?" Harry said again. He was getting impatient.

I hesitated. If I had a tattoo *there*, it would mean no more swimming in the ocean with just my trunks on. I'd have to wear a shirt. Of course, I could always sit in a beach chair with Dad. He never takes his shirt off either when we go to the beach. He just sits in his beach chair doing physics problems, while Mom grades papers.

I'd miss swimming in the ocean, but it would be worth it.

I looked Harry straight in the eye. "I want it on my chest!" I said.

Chapter Two

"TAKE off your shirt," Harry said, "and lie down."

I did as I was told. The table smelled of cheap cologne and sweat. This was the real world!

"You've got good skin," Harry said. "It'll take the dye real good."

"Thanks, Harry."

Harry was examining my chest carefully. "You know, the older I get, the younger you sailors look. Why, I had a sailor in here yesterday I'd have sworn should have been in the sixth grade!"

"Oh, really? How strange."

Harry began swabbing my chest with alcohol. It was cold and the fumes were making me dizzy. "We don't want any infection, do we?"

"Infection?" I said woozily.

"Don't worry," Harry assured me. "One sailor in a million gets an infected tattoo."

"What number am I?"

"Huh?" Harry said, then added, "Oh, I get it. Ha! Ha! You're not anywhere near the magic number."

"That's good," I said with a sigh, but I thought, I must be out of my mind. I was almost ready to jump off the table and run out of the tattoo parlor, when suddenly Loretta's face passed before my eyes. *"There is absolutely nothing distinctive about you, Hershell Cobwell!"* she screamed. Then she stuck out her tongue.

"Are you ready?" Harry asked.

"I'm ready," I said determinedly. I closed my eyes.

"You'll feel a little pain when I stick your skin with the needle."

Needle? I didn't know anything about a needle! My life started passing before my eyes. I can't stand pain! "AAAAAAAAAAIIIIIIIIIEEEEE-EEEEE!"

"Oh, no, not another screamer," Harry muttered.

I sat up. "I'm sorry. I don't know what came over me."

"Lie back down!" Harry commanded.

I did as I was told.

"We'll try again," Harry said.

"I'll try to do better this time, Harry," I promised. "I really do want this tattoo."

Harry started with the needle again.

I started taking short panting breaths. "Ah! Ah! Ah! Ah! Ah! Ah! Ah! Ah! Ah! Ah!"

"You sound like my dog," Harry said.

"I'm sorry, Harry, really I am, but it does help to kill the pain."

"You know," Harry said, continuing to stick me with his needle, "I remember a time when the Navy attracted *real* men. What's the matter? Don't they get tattoos anymore? All I seem to get are the screamers!"

"You must be ah! ah! ah! ah! thinking of the ah!

ah! ah! ah! Army or the ah! ah! ah! ah! Marines," I managed to say. Then I passed out.

"Wake up, sailor," Harry said. "It's all done!"

I opened my eyes. My chest felt like it was on fire. I couldn't believe how much it hurt.

"You can sit up," Harry added. "I'm finished."

"Are you sure?"

"Of course, I'm sure. The rose is beautiful and 'MOTHER' is spelled perfect."

"No," I said, wincing from the pain, "are you sure I can sit up?"

"Yeah, yeah, sailor, just try it!" Harry was getting a little testy, I could tell.

I tried to sit up, but I fell back quickly, because I was stretching my chest skin too much. "I don't think I can, Harry. It hurts too much!"

"Keep it down! I've got some customers waiting. Now, just be a good swabbie and get up." Harry was beginning to grind his teeth.

"You'll have to help me," I whispered back.

"All right, all right," Harry whispered, "but if I were you, I wouldn't let the rest of the Navy see me in this condition. They'd run you out of San Diego, man!"

Harry helped me off the table and handed me my shirt.

There were two sailors sitting in a couple of the chairs. "Let me see it," one of them said.

I looked up. "What?"

"Let's see your tattoo, man," the other one said.

I gritted my teeth and forced myself to straighten up. Pain shot through me and I felt faint, but I remained standing.

Harry was beaming.

"Man, that's beautiful!" one of the sailors said.

"That rose looks real," the other one said. "That's for me! Only I want my girl's name across *my* chest."

The pain forced me to bend back over. I slowly began putting on my shirt. Harry helped me with the sleeves.

"Thanks, Harry," I said, then I started to leave.

But Harry stopped me. "Haven't you forgotten something, sailor?"

"Oh, yeah, my jacket." I started toward the coat rack by the door.

"No, no, I mean my fifteen dollars!"

"Oh, yeah, that, too." I got out my wallet, took out fifteen dollars, and handed it to Harry. Now all I had left was a pocketful of quarters.

"If I do a really super job," Harry added, "some sailors like to show their appreciation with a tip." His hand was still out.

"How much do you usually get?" I asked.

"A dollar, two dollars," Harry said. "It just depends on how much they appreciate my work."

"I think I appreciate it one dollar." I took four quarters out of my pocket and handed them to Harry. "I don't have too much money left."

"You sailors should take better care of your money," Harry said, then he turned to his two new customers and said, "Well, fellows, what'll it be?"

I slowly walked out of the shop.

My shirt was rubbing against the tattoo, but it didn't seem to be hurting as much as it had been.

In fact, I was even able to straighten up a little by the time I left the Deep Blue Sea Locker Club.

I stood outside the entrance, tucking in my shirt and wondering what in the world I was going to do next.

It was almost two o'clock. Señora Diaz's Spanish class was just about over. I hated to have missed it. I liked Spanish.

I put on my jacket and started walking. A Chicano passed me. *"Buenas tardes,"* I said. If I couldn't be in Spanish class, I could at least get a little practical experience.

The Chicano said something in Spanish, but it was a word that I had never heard before.

A couple of sailors were on the sidewalk ahead of me, walking in the same direction. I was walking faster than they were, so I passed them. Somehow, in the daylight, I felt exposed for what I really was: a fraud.

"Hey, buddy!" one of them said to my back.

I stopped. I've had it now, I thought. I turned around slowly and tried to slouch. "Yeah?"

"What ship you off of?" the first sailor asked.

I grinned. "Uh, uh, we just got in." I started to open my shirt and show them my tattoo. Then it hit me that they might want me to pal around San Diego with them, so I added, "Well, uh, uh, I guess I'd better be going. I, uh, uh, have to see my girl."

"Lucky guy," they both said.

I turned away from them and headed down the sidewalk, but I could feel the pride inside me swelling the tattoo on my chest to twice its size.

I turned the corner and found the bus stop. I looked at the schedule, but I couldn't decide which one I needed. I'd never had to ride a bus from downtown by myself before.

Then I noticed a lady with a shopping bag leaning against a store window. I walked over to her. "Excuse me."

She stopped chewing her gum and looked at me. I had never seen eyelashes so long or hair so blonde. She had on more makeup than Mom wears in a whole year. "Yeah, kid, whadda you want?"

Kid, she had called me. I couldn't believe what I was hearing, not after fooling a man of the world like Harry and all of those sailors. I forgot all about the bus schedule.

"What makes you think I'm a kid?" I demanded.

"Look at you!" Her lips sort of formed in a snarl. "You're a shrimp!"

Well, there was no way I could let this pass and still retain what little dignity I had managed to keep all of these years. I had to do it. If the guys on television could do it, I could, too!

I ripped open my shirt!

That really startled her. I thought for a minute she was going to scream.

But when she saw my tattoo, she calmed down. "Well, get you, honey. I never would have believed it. My, my, the Navy's really taking them young these days."

"You'd better believe it!" I started rebuttoning my shirt, but two of the buttons had popped off.

The woman started to say something else, but a bus hissed to a stop behind us. I turned and looked at it, then I looked back at her. She had a funny expression on her face. I had seen that look before in the movies, but I didn't know what it meant.

"I think that's my bus," I said.

"That's too bad."

"Huh?"

She puckered her lips. "Maybe I'll see you around sometime."

"Uh, well, uh, yeah, well, maybe," I managed to say. Then I walked over to the bus.

"Hey, kid!" the driver yelled. "Did you get your school report done?"

I cringed. It was the same driver who had dropped me off this morning.

I hurriedly stepped onto the bus. I could feel my face turning red. Had the woman heard? I couldn't bear to look at her. She was probably laughing her head off at me right now. But I wanted to remember her face the way it had been when she first saw my tattoo.

The bus had already gone two blocks before I realized I didn't have time to think about that woman now.

I had a decision to make. I had to decide whether to get off the bus at Jackson Elementary School or to ride it all the way home.

School was out at ten after two. It was now two-fifteen. Most of the guys in my class would be going to baseball practice.

I had tried out for baseball. But I hadn't made the team. It wasn't that I wasn't good, really, it was just that somebody had left my name off the final list. Coach Nottingham had said that I could file a formal protest if I wanted to, but when he explained the procedure, it all seemed too complicated.

Of course, I could go on home and watch television. That would be the easiest thing to do. I wouldn't have to face anybody that way.

Dad was at his office and Mom was at the university.

Loretta wouldn't be there, either. She was probably in the library working on one of her research papers.

I always enjoyed that time of day when I had the house completely to myself.

I looked out the bus window again. Jackson Elementary School was coming into view. I now knew which choice I had to make.

I hadn't suffered all morning at Painless Harry's Tattoo Parlour just to sit in front of a television set the rest of my life!

I pressed the rubber lining that rang the bell to let the driver know I wanted to get off.

If I was ever going to be distinctive, I'd have to show my tattoo to the people who counted.

I'd start with the baseball team.

Chapter Three

WHEN I got to the baseball diamond behind the school, I was surprised to find a game in progress. It was the Purple Dragons against the Black Panthers. The Dragons are the fifth-grade team and the Panthers are the sixth-grade team. Purple and black are our school colors.

According to the scoreboard, the Dragons were ahead seven runs to two.

Coach Nottingham and the Panthers were huddled just like a football team in their dugout across the field. I had heard that Coach Nottingham would rather be coaching football than baseball.

I started walking toward them.

"We're going to win this game, men," Coach Nottingham was shouting, "because the most important thing in winning is having good material and we've got good material!"

"They've got better!" Spunky Madison shouted.

"Aw, keep quiet, Spunky!" the rest of the team shouted.

"I'm here to help you boys reach your full potential," Coach Nottingham continued.

"We've already reached it!" Spunky shouted again.

"Aw, keep quiet, Spunky!" the rest of the team shouted again.

"It's my duty to build the *esprit de corps*," Coach Nottingham shouted.

"I don't speak French," Spunky shouted.

"Hi, fellows," I said.

Everybody looked up.

"What are you doing here, Cobwell?" Spunky demanded. "You didn't make the team."

While everybody was looking at me, waiting for an answer, I ripped open my shirt and showed them my tattoo.

All their mouths dropped open, but Coach Nottingham's dropped open the farthest. "What *is* that, Cobwell?" he asked.

"It's a tattoo. I just got it."

"Where'd you get it?" Spunky asked.

"At the foot of Broadway," I replied.

"Man, I'm impressed," Spunky said.

The rest of the team murmured their agreement.

"Did it hurt?" Spunky asked.

"Naw."

Coach Nottingham, Spunky, and the rest of the team looked at me in disbelief.

"Well, it might have hurt a little at first," I said, "but it feels just great now."

"Boy, you must be real tough, Cobwell," Coach Nottingham said.

I sort of shrugged. "How's the game going?" I asked nonchalantly.

"We're losing," Coach Nottingham replied.

"Too bad."

Coach Nottingham looked at me for a minute,

then he said, “Didn’t you go out for the team, Cobwell?”

“Yessir, but my name got left off the final list.”

“Really?” Coach Nottingham exclaimed. Then I saw a light go on in his head. He rehuddled the team for a minute. Then he unhuddled them. “How would you like to play baseball for the Panthers?” he asked me.

“Sure. Why not?”

“What position do you play?” Coach Nottingham asked.

“I play all positions.”

Coach Nottingham and the team looked surprised, but nobody on the team said anything.

Coach Nottingham said, “We need a pitcher!”

“Hey, what about me?” Spunky shouted.

“We’re five runs behind,” Coach Nottingham said. “I’m calling you in!”

“I don’t have a uniform,” I said.

“That’s all right. You can use Spunky’s cap,” Coach Nottingham said. “That’s good enough for now.”

Spunky threw his cap to me and I put it on. It was too small, but I wasn’t about to complain.

Then *our* team ran back out onto the field.

My shirt was still open and my tattoo was showing.

The Dragons’ first batter up was their pitcher, Melvin Bookman. I looked him straight in the eye. I was going to try to split the heart of the plate.

I tried to visualize the path of the ball. I moved my fingers slightly to the right of my fastball grip and pulled over and straight down on the ball. I bent my elbow slightly and brought it closer to my body. Then I drew back and released the ball. It was a perfect pitch.

But the Dragons' pitcher just stood there.

"STRIKE ONE!" the umpire yelled.

The guy hadn't even swung at the ball. He was staring at *me*. Actually, he was staring at my *tattoo*.

In fact, the whole Dragons team was standing up staring at my tattoo.

I decided to throw a curve ball next.

I threw it. But the batter just stood there again, staring at my tattoo.

"STRIKE TWO!"

Coach Lemons, the coach of the Dragons, pulled the batter off and started talking to him.

The batter pointed to me.

Coach Lemons threw up his hands and walked back to the dugout.

The batter walked back up to the plate.

I was beginning to feel powerful.

I threw a sidearm sinker.

Still nothing from the batter.

"STRIKE THREE! YOU'R-R-R-R-R-RE OUT!" the umpire shouted.

Our team cheered.

So did the three sixth-grade cheerleaders who were standing on the sidelines now.

They waved at me and jumped up and down and giggled.

I couldn't believe it. Lori Beth McPherson, Juli Rae Knight, and Cindi Kaye Tankersley! Some of the most beautiful girls at Jackson Elementary School and they were cheering for me!

I struck out the catcher and the first baseman,

mainly because they just stood there staring at my tattoo.

Coach Lemons was pulling out what was left of his hair.

While we were running in to have our turn at bat, he had a shouting match with Coach Nottingham.

I couldn't hear what they were saying, but Coach Nottingham was shrugging his shoulders and grinning a lot.

I was up first at bat.

I walked up to the plate. My shirt was flapping in the breeze. My tattoo seemed larger than life.

A crowd had begun gathering in the stands.

Two more cheerleaders had joined Lori, Juli, and Cindi: Debbi Jean Linz and Terri Sue Wainwright! Debbi had just been named Miss Pre-Teen San Diego and Terri was the first runner-up. I didn't think I could stand it. I looked over at them. They were all jumping up and down and waving at *me*. I waved back.

Then I looked at the Dragons' pitcher. It was still Melvin Bookman. And he was still staring at my tattoo. But now our roles were reversed.

His first pitch was four feet off home plate.

"BALL ONE!" the umpire shouted.

His second pitch was eight feet off home plate.

"BALL TWO!"

His third pitch went into the stands behind me.

"BALL THREE!"

His fourth pitch disappeared over the fence.

"BALL FOUR!"

Melvin had never taken his eyes off my chest.

I walked to first base to the cheers of Lori, Juli,

Cindi, Debbi, and Terri, and to the cheers of the team and of the crowd in the stands that had now grown to about fifty people.

Actually, I was sort of disappointed, though. I knew that I could have hit a home run if only Melvin had been able to get a pitch over home plate.

But Melvin was still so stunned by my tattoo that he also walked the catcher and the first baseman.

When he walked the second baseman, I walked in and scored.

The cheerleaders cheered.

The crowd in the stands roared.

Coach Nottingham and the Panthers surrounded me and said all kinds of nice things.

It was Dragons seven, Panthers three.

Coach Lemons went out onto the mound to talk to Melvin. He was waving his hands around in the air a lot.

Frannie Tompkins rushed up to me just as I was heading for the dugout. Frannie was a pushy fifth grader who tried to make everybody think she was in the sixth, but she was also one of the photographers for *The Tattler*, the Jackson Elementary School yearbook.

"Could I take a picture of you, Hershell?" Frannie asked. She waved her camera at me. It was one she had gotten free with a subscription to a magazine. "I'd like for you to be holding your bat, but don't let it cover up your tattoo."

"Okay." I struck a pose like the ones I had seen in *Sports Illustrated*. "How's this?"

Frannie looked through her camera lens. Then

she looked at my tattoo. Her eyes became glazed and she remained motionless.

"Are you going to take my picture, Frannie?"

"Oh, uh, yes, yes, I was just thinking. We need some background. Do you have any suggestions?"

"What about the other members of the team?" I suggested magnanimously.

"Great idea, Hershell." Frannie gave me a big smile. "But what else should I expect from somebody with your brains?"

I shrugged. Then I called Coach Nottingham and the rest of the team over. I also motioned to Lori, Juli, Cindi, Debbi, and Terri. They ran up screaming and yelling and doing their cartwheels all over the place. It was so noisy that I couldn't hear the directions that Frannie was giving me.

"Girls, girls, calm down!" I said.

"Sure, Hershell," Debbi squealed. I guess she was the spokeswoman for the group.

Frannie lined up Coach Nottingham and the other players from the team, and then she put me in front of them.

Then she put Lori, Juli, and Cindi on one side and Debbi and Terri on the other side. Then she looked through her camera lens again.

"This isn't going to work," she said. "It's uneven. There are three cheerleaders on one side and two on the other!"

"Where's Patti?" Lori demanded.

"Here I am!" Patti squealed. She was running across the infield toward us. She started doing her cartwheels and tumbling act as she ran.

The crowd cheered.

Finally, Patti reached us. "Hi, Hershell!" she

shouted breathlessly. "I got here as soon as I heard the news!"

"Hi, Patti!" I couldn't believe it. Patti Carroll Mason was the most beautiful girl in the world!

She stood next to Lori, Juli, and Cindi, because they were all friends.

Frannie looked at Patti and said, "You're supposed to be on the other side."

Patti gave Frannie a puzzled look. Then she turned to me. "What does she mean, Hershell?"

"She wants you next to Debbi and Terri," I explained.

"But Lori, Juli, and Cindi are my friends," Patti said. "I want to stay where I am!"

"But you're *unbalanced*!" Frannie cried. "There are four cheerleaders on one side and two cheerleaders on the other!"

"Well?" Patti said. She intended to stand her ground. I had heard that she always got her way.

I looked at Patti. I made sure that my tattoo was showing. "Do it for me," I said.

Patti sighed, then she hurried to the other side and stood next to Debbi and Terri.

"Thanks," I said.

Patti sighed again.

"Ready?" Frannie shouted.

"Ready!" we all shouted back. Then we smiled.

Frannie looked into the lens of her camera and the clicking began.

Then she shouted, "I need some action shots now, girls! Do some yells!"

Lori, Juli, Cindi, Debbi, Terri, and Patti broke from their pose with me and the rest of the team and started jumping up and down and turning cartwheels and somersaults all over the place.

Then Patti's feet hit me in the chest and knocked me down. "Oh, Hershell, are you all right?" she screamed as she helped me up. She was near tears.

"I'm fine," I managed to say. Actually I was writhing in pain. She had kicked me right in the middle of my tattoo.

"Oh, I'm so sorry," Patti said with a sob.

"Don't be. It was just an accident."

"But you of all people, Hershell!" Patti said. "How could I do that to *you*?"

"Accidents happen." I gritted my teeth and smiled. Actually, the throbbing had started to go away.

Patti's eyes were on my tattoo.

Just then Coach Lemons stormed up. He had the umpire with him. "All right, Nottingham," he said to the coach, "let's get this game going again." He gave me a dirty look.

The catcher, the first baseman, and the second baseman ran back out to the bases. The rest of our team headed for the dugout.

The cheerleaders ran to the sidelines.

Frannie ran toward the school building. "I need to get these pictures developed right away!" she shouted over her shoulder to me. "I want to use them in this year's *Tattler*!"

All of a sudden I realized what I had done. I had let somebody take photographic evidence of my tattoo!

I couldn't believe how dumb I had been! What if my parents saw those pictures? What would I do then? Of course, I had planned to tell them about the tattoo. Eventually.

"Frannie! Wait up!" I cried.

But Frannie had already reached the school building and was going through a side door.

"Play ball!" the umpire shouted.

I looked around helplessly. What have I gotten myself into? I wondered. I wanted to be distinctive, but I only wanted certain people to know about it for now.

I looked out toward the field.

The Dragons had a new pitcher: Elbert Mackie. He was a tough kid. He was always trying to beat me up.

Harry Tankersley, our third baseman, walked up to the plate. He looked nervous. I knew I had to do something.

I stood where Elbert could see me. I made sure that my shirt was open enough so that the tattoo was showing. Elbert started staring at it.

My old confidence was coming back. I probably didn't have anything to worry about. *The Tattler* didn't come out until the end of the year, and by that time I would have figured out just exactly how I was going to break the news of my tattoo to my parents.

Elbert's first pitch was wide to the right.

"BALL ONE!" the umpire shouted.

His second pitch was wide to the left.

"BALL TWO!"

His third pitch was low and inside.

"BALL THREE!"

The wind blew my shirt together, hiding my tattoo. Elbert's pitch was right on target but Harry hit a grand-slam home run.

Everybody went wild.

It was Dragons seven, Panthers seven.

When things settled down, I stood up and opened my shirt again.

But the umpire made me go back to the dugout while he and Coach Lemons studied the rule book.

Everybody struck out after that.

The Dragons came in and we went out.

I took my place on the pitcher's mound and opened my shirt. Coach Lemons looked up from the rule book but didn't say anything.

I struck out the second baseman, the third baseman, and the shortstop all in a row.

We went in and the Dragons came out.

It was now the bottom of the ninth and I was up at bat.

I stood at the plate, letting the breeze flap open my shirt.

The Dragons had another new pitcher. It was Vilnius Tartu. It was rumored that Vilnius was really older than he said he was. He was looking me straight in the eye.

I moved so he could see my tattoo better. But the wind kept blowing my shirt together. It was hard holding the bat with one hand and my shirt open with the other.

Vilnius threw a drop ball.

"STRIKE ONE!" the umpire shouted.

Vilnius threw a curve ball.

"STRIKE TWO!"

The crowd gasped.

Coach Nottingham and the rest of the team looked tense.

The wind kept blowing my shirt together.

Then I moved away from the plate and did the

only thing I could do under the circumstances. I took off my shirt.

The crowd cheered.

I made a complete circle at home plate.

The crowd cheered again.

Lori, Juli, Cindi, Debbi, Terri, and Patti did simultaneous somersaults.

Vilnius threw another pitch and I hit it into left field for a home run.

It was now Panthers eight, Dragons seven, and the game was over.

The crowd went wild and rushed out onto the field.

Lori, Juli, Cindi, Debbi, Terri, and Patti formed a circle around me and the rest of the Panthers formed a circle around them and we all ran for the dugout.

"This calls for a celebration!" Coach Nottingham shouted. "I have never before beaten one of Coach Lemons' teams!"

The team cheered.

The cheerleaders cheered again. Then they started doing cartwheels in the dugout.

"Next week, team, we play the Westside Bombers," Coach Nottingham continued. "They were California State Champions last year, and we're going to beat them because we've got Hershell Cobwell!"

Everybody cheered.

"Pizza's on me!" Coach Nottingham shouted.

Everybody cheered again.

"And now, men, to the showers!" Coach Nottingham shouted.

Lori, Juli, Cindi, Debbi, Terri, and Patti

shouted, "We'll meet you at Mr. Perugi's Pizza Palace, Hershell!"

"Okay!" I shouted back.

Actually, what I wanted to do more than anything now was to go home and think about all the other ways I was going to conquer Jackson Elementary School.

Chapter Four

I COULDN'T believe how exhausting it was to be popular. I just wasn't up to this physically. I'd probably have to start working out with weights.

By the time I finally got home, I was tired and sweaty and full of Mr. Perugi's pizza. I was also a little nervous. I had invited all the members of the baseball team over to my house to talk about our next game. Actually, Spunky Madison had suggested it, and I had thought it was a good idea, even though I had never done anything like that before. But I told them to give me about an hour before they came over.

I had hoped to walk home alone from the pizza palace, because I needed some time to think about how I was going to break the news of the meeting to my parents, but just as I was leaving, Patti Carroll Mason grabbed me and insisted that she walk home with me. How could I refuse the most beautiful girl in the world?

But now, standing outside the front door of my house, I wished I had refused. I needed more time to think about what I was going to say.

For the time being, at least, I didn't have to worry about my tattoo. All the players on the team were turning out to be real regular guys. When I asked them not to say anything about the tattoo in front of Loretta or my parents, they all said they wouldn't. I could tell they understood the situation. In fact, several of them agreed that their parents would have killed them if they had gotten a tattoo. That made me feel a lot better.

I tried to turn the knob on the front door of my house, but it kept slipping in my sweaty palm. Finally, I got it open.

I found Mom and Dad and Loretta in the kitchen. They were eating dinner in silence.

"Hello," I said.

Everybody looked up, startled.

"Where have you been?" Loretta demanded.

"Yes," Mom said, "where *have* you been?"

"It's unlike you not to be here when we all get home," Dad added.

"Yeah, you're always watching television when I get home," Loretta said. "Why weren't you watching television, Hershell?"

I looked down to make sure that my tattoo was covered. It was. "I was . . . out."

"Out?" Loretta said. "Out *where*?"

"I was just out. I was playing baseball with some friends. I'm on the team now."

"Friends?" Loretta said. "I didn't know you had any friends. Where'd you get friends? You've never had any friends before!"

"Now, Loretta," Dad said, "Hershell might just have a friend . . . or two." He looked at me. "Do you, son?"

"Yes, I do," I replied.

"Well, wash up, Hershell," Mom said. "Your dinner's getting cold."

"I've already eaten. I had pizza over at Mr. Perugi's Pizza Palace with the rest of the team."

"Well, you can at least sit down and tell us how your day at school went," Dad said.

"School?" I said.

"See!" Loretta said. "He can't even remember where he was today. How can a person like that have friends?"

The telephone spared me the rest of the conversation.

"I'll get it," Loretta shouted. She jumped up from the table and grabbed the receiver. "Hello!" Then she gulped twice and turned pale. "You're one of *Hershell's* friends?" she gasped.

Mom and Dad looked at me.

I smiled, walked to the telephone, and took the receiver from Loretta.

"I can't believe that somebody would actually call him on the telephone," Loretta said, as she sat back down slowly. "He never gets telephone calls."

I flipped on the telephone loudspeaker so everybody could hear the conversation. "Hello," I said.

"Hello," the voice on the telephone said. "This is Maxwell Haverford Brown. Of course you've heard of me."

"I, uh, well, I'm not sure," I stammered. I was trying desperately to think. I didn't want to blow this.

"I'm the smartest boy in the sixth grade," Maxwell said. The tone of his voice made me feel as though I weren't very smart if I didn't know that.

"Oh, yes, yes, *that* Maxwell Haverford Brown!"

I could almost see him smiling. I looked over at Mom, Dad, and Loretta. Their mouths were open.

"You are clearly, next to me, the most original thinker at Jackson Elementary School. I can't believe I've never heard of you," Maxwell said. "I'd like to come over and visit with you for a few minutes."

"He's got to be kidding!" Loretta cried.

I covered the mouth of the receiver with my hand and gave her a dirty look. Then I said, "Of course. When did you want to come over?" Then it hit me! He'd want to see my tattoo. He'd ask me about it in front of Mom, Dad, and Loretta. I couldn't let him come over to my house now. Besides, I had already invited the guys on the baseball team. What would they say if I had the smartest boy in the sixth grade here?

"What about now?" Maxwell said. "Have you dined yet?"

"Uh, well, yes, I have, but . . ."

"Then I'll come on over."

"Well, I . . ." I tried to say, but Maxwell had already hung up. Then I broke out in an even colder sweat. What if Maxwell had said something over the *telephone* about my tattoo? Loretta and my parents would have heard it, and everything would be over. I had been so concerned with impressing them, I'd had a momentary lapse of good judgement.

I sighed. For the moment, I was safe, but I'd have to watch myself and not let that happen again.

"There's something very strange going on here," Loretta said. "None of the smart kids would have talked to someone like you when I was in the sixth grade!"

I turned to face Loretta. "Times have changed. We're living in a more democratic society, Loretta. Why should there be anything strange going on just because the smartest kid in the sixth grade wants to come over and visit me?"

"Because, Hershell Cobwell, you have never ever before in your entire life had any friends, that's why, and especially not somebody like Maxwell Haverford Brown." Loretta's eyes narrowed to slits. "What have you been doing?" she demanded. "That's what I want to know!"

"Now, Loretta," Dad said soothingly, "if Hershell has found himself a friend, you shouldn't castigate him for it."

"I'm not castigating him for it, Father, I'm just trying to determine exactly how he did it. Something is just not right here. But mark my word, I'll get to the bottom of this yet!"

I bet you will, too, Loretta, I thought, but not until I'm already the most distinctive boy at Jackson Elementary School, and then it won't matter.

What I had to worry about now was how to keep Maxwell Haverford Brown from asking about the tattoo in front of my family, yet still impress him enough that he'd want to pal around with me. I'd always heard that if you palled around with the smartest kid in the class, teachers just automatically gave you good grades. It was exciting to think about.

Loretta was looking at me. "Yes," she said slowly, "if I just think about this long enough, it'll all come to me. If it concerns Hershell, it can't be too complicated." She turned to Mom and Dad. "But first I have to finish my math problems," she added. "I am the most advanced person in my class!"

The doorbell rang.

"I'll get it," I said. "It's probably my *friend* Maxwell Haverford Brown, the smartest boy in the sixth grade." I was really getting into the swing of this.

But when I opened the door, the person standing there didn't look anything like how I had pictured Maxwell Haverford Brown. In fact, this person sort of looked like a girl.

Whoever this was was dressed in strange-looking clothes. Her pants were leather and her shirt looked like it had once been a parachute. She also had on very dark glasses, and in one hand she was holding a scrapbook.

"Maxwell?" I said.

"I'm Elisabeth La Chazze," she replied.

La Chazze. That name sounded familiar. "Oh, yes! Your brother must be the one whose picture wasn't in the yearbook last year, either," I said. "Jason?"

"Ah, yes, dear, dear Jason," Elisabeth said. "Unfortunately, he still has a lot to learn about the importance of publicity shots." She looked at me. "May I come in?"

"Well, I guess so."

I stood aside and let Elisabeth come into the house. Actually, she sort of pranced in and continued to whirl and strike poses all around the living room.

"Won't you sit down?" I said.

"Thank you," Elisabeth said. She sat down on the couch.

I sat down next to her. "Is there something you wanted to talk to me about?"

"Yes, Hershell, there is. I am sure you are aware that I star in all the dramatic productions at Jackson."

"Oh, yes, I've seen you in every All-School Play since kindergarten. You were always very good."

Elisabeth smiled. I had obviously said the right thing. She stood up and pranced over to a chair and sat down.

"This is really a thrill for me, having you in my house," I said.

"I know," Elisabeth said.

"You said you wanted to talk to me about something. If it's about my tat . . ."

"Hershell, did your . . . uh, *friend* arrive?" Mom was standing in the doorway of the living room. She looked over at Elisabeth. She seemed a little puzzled at seeing a girl, but she said, "How do you do? I'm Dr. Cobwell, Hershell's mother. We're so glad that he has a friend."

"Please, Mom," I said.

Elisabeth stood up, pranced her way over to Mom, and curtsied. "I'm Elisabeth La Chazze, and I star in all the dramatic productions at Jackson."

"How nice," Mom said.

"Who's in here?" Loretta had come into the living room and was standing, hands on hips.

"This is Elisabeth La Chazze, Loretta," I said.

Loretta looked at Elisabeth. "You look very familiar."

"I know," Elisabeth said.

"I have a very high IQ," Loretta continued, "and my mother's a doctor and my father's a doctor." She turned and looked at me with disgust again, then she looked back at Elisabeth. "Which one of us *three* are you here to see?"

"Actually, I'm here to see Hershell." Elisabeth looked at me. "I want him to star opposite me in this year's All-School Play."

I couldn't believe what I had just heard. I didn't want to be in any play!

"Hershell?" Loretta screamed. She had a panic-stricken look on her face.

"Yes," Elisabeth continued, seemingly oblivious to Loretta's outburst. "I am a very good judge of dramatic talent and I feel that one day Hershell Cobwell's name will be up in lights on Broadway!"

"How nice," Mom said.

Loretta looked like she was about to choke.

"What's going on in here?" Dad had come into the living room.

Elisabeth looked up, then she struck a pose and held out her hand for Dad to shake.

The doorbell rang.

"I'll get it!" I shouted.

When I opened the door, standing there was a tall, skinny person with glasses.

He held out his hand. "I'm Maxwell Haverford Brown and I'm the smartest boy in the sixth grade," he said. "May I come in?"

"Of course! But I'd rather not talk about my you-know-what in front of you-know-who, if you know what I mean. I'm planning to surprise them with it later."

Then I led Maxwell into the living room.

Mom, Dad, and Loretta were all seated on the sofa. Elisabeth had started showing them her scrapbook.

I turned back to Maxwell. "Have a seat."

Maxwell sat down in a chair.

I sat opposite him. I looked nervously toward my parents and Loretta. "Did you want to see me about anything special?" I whispered to Maxwell.

"I just wanted to talk to you first," Maxwell said. "I can tell a lot about a person's IQ from the way he talks."

"Well, like I said, I'd rather not talk about you-know-what. Could I talk about something else?"

"Actually, I'd like for you to talk about Spinoza, Voltaire, and Denmark," Maxwell said. "Light subjects like that. We'll get into the heavier subjects tomorrow." He smiled. "I can't believe that I've finally found somebody smart enough to talk to me."

I was beginning to sweat. But the doorbell saved me. "Excuse me," I said.

When I opened the door, I recognized Hal Hall, the biggest punk at Jackson Elementary School. He was dressed in black leather pants and a black leather jacket. He was also wearing a black leather cap with studs. He was holding a motorcycle magazine in his hand. I had heard rumors around school that Hal had once actually talked to a member of the Hell's Angels.

Hal looked from side to side, then said, "You gonna let me in or what?"

"Sure!" I had always been impressed by Hal's toughness. "I'm honored to have you in my home."

"Yeah, yeah," Hal said.

I led him into the living room.

Mom and Dad were still looking at Elisabeth's scrapbook.

But Maxwell was now talking to Loretta about physics.

"Here, Hal, you can sit down here . . ." I started to say. But then I noticed the grease spots on his pants. "Better not sit down there," I added hurriedly. "Mom and Dad would be furious if you got that chair dirty."

Hal sneered. "What's a little motorcycle grease? We have it all over our furniture at home. My parents are used to it, man!"

"Well, actually, I wouldn't mind, if it were up to me, but you know how some moms and dads are." I looked around. "How about that plastic chair over there? We can wash that one off."

Hal strutted over and sat down. "Me and the other guys heard about you today, man. We think it's great. You're one tough fellow and we may want you to hang out with us."

I couldn't believe what I was hearing. "You mean you want me to be a punk like you?"

Hal shrugged. "We haven't decided for sure." He looked me straight in the eye. "I've been sent over by the rest of the punks to size you up. Show me your tattoo!"

I almost choked. "Uh, Hal," I whispered, "could you kind of keep it down? You see, I haven't had a chance to tell my folks yet. You know how it is. There just hasn't been a good time."

But before Hal could say anything, the doorbell rang again.

I looked around. Nobody was paying attention

to me or it. "Just a minute, Hal. There's somebody at the door."

But Hal had already moved. He was sitting next to Mom and Dad on our good sofa and making faces at Elisabeth.

I walked to the front door and opened it. There stood Coach Nottingham, Spunky Madison, and Harry Tankersley.

"Where's the rest of the team?" I asked.

"They ate too much pizza and threw up all over the place," Spunky replied. "Mr. Perugi is making them clean it up."

I turned and looked back toward the living room. I couldn't believe there were so many people in the house. I wasn't quite sure how much longer I could keep my tattoo a secret from my parents and Loretta with all this going on. I was just sure that somebody would slip and give me away.

"Aren't you going to ask us in, Cobwell?" Harry said. "I thought we were going to have a meeting."

"Gee, I don't know, guys." I nodded my head toward the living room. "Things are getting out of hand." I hesitated for a couple of minutes. "But I guess if you want to come inside . . ."

"That's okay," Spunky said. "I think I'm about to throw up. I guess I'd better go on home."

"Yeah, me, too," Harry said.

"I was going to go over some game plans with you," Coach Nottingham said, "but that can wait until tomorrow."

"Thanks, guys. I knew you'd understand."

Coach Nottingham punched me on the shoulder. "Glad to have you on our team, Cobwell."

"Where's your bathroom, Hershell?" Spunky

cried. "I don't think I'm going to make it until I get home." He had one hand over his stomach and another over his mouth.

"Use the bushes, Madison," Coach Nottingham said.

Spunky jumped off the porch and headed for the bushes at the corner of the house.

"Wait for me!" Harry cried.

Coach Nottingham shook his head. "I've got a lot of things to discuss with you, Cobwell. You have a very bright future in baseball at Jackson Elementary School."

"Thanks, Coach," I said. Then I shut the front door and turned around. Nobody had been paying any attention to what I had been doing.

The doorbell rang again. This time it was Patti Carroll Mason. Behind her on the porch stood Lori, Juli, Cindi, Debbi, and Terri.

"Hi, Hershell," Patti said.

"Hi, Patti. What are all of you doing here?"

"Oh, Hershell, we just wanted to be a part of the team meeting. May we come inside?"

"Well, there really isn't going to be . . ."

"I want to go steady with you, Hershell," Patti interrupted.

"So do we!" all the other girls cried.

"But I'm the Head Cheerleader!" Patti declared.

"So what!" all the other girls cried.

I had to do something quick. "Listen, girls," I said. "I'm going to be kind of busy with baseball for a while. I probably won't have time to go steady with anyone."

The girls all looked at me.

"Well, as soon as baseball season is over, you're

mine!" Patti shouted. Then she started down the steps of the porch.

"No he's not!" the other girls shouted and started down the steps after her.

I noticed that a crowd had now gathered on the sidewalk. I recognized them as kids in the neighborhood who went to Jackson Elementary School.

"There he is!" somebody shouted.

"Take off your shirt!" somebody else shouted.

I checked to make sure nobody in my house would see me, then I opened my shirt. The light from the porch illuminated the tattoo.

The crowd cheered.

I turned to see if anybody in the house had heard the noise. That's when I saw Elisabeth whirling and posing her way toward me, followed by Mom and Dad.

I hurriedly buttoned my shirt.

"I'll talk to you tomorrow, Hershell," Elisabeth said when she reached me. "I'll tell you all about your role in the All-School Play. I'm too tired now."

"Uh, well, uh, okay, Elisabeth," I said. I knew it wouldn't do any good to protest now. I stepped aside and let her make her way out onto the porch, down the steps, and into the crowd that was still in front of our house.

"What are all those kids doing out there?" Mom asked.

"Beats me," I mumbled.

"Good luck in the Student-of-the-Year election, Maxwell," Loretta said. She and Maxwell had also come to the front door.

Hal was standing behind them. Now he was making faces at Maxwell.

"Thanks, Loretta," Maxwell said. Then he turned to me. "Keep thinking, Hershell," he said, "and I'll talk to you tomorrow at school."

"Okay," I said.

"Sorry about all that motorcycle grease on your good couch, Hershell," Hal said, "but it comes with the territory." He winked. "You'll get used to it."

"What are all those kids doing in front of our house?" Dad asked.

"I asked the same question," Mom said.

I hurriedly closed the front door. "They're probably just out for an evening stroll."

Mom, Dad, and Loretta just stood there, looking at me. They all had funny expressions on their faces.

"Kids don't take evening strolls, Hershell," Mom said.

"I bet it's a gang fight," Dad added.

"Something very strange has been happening here tonight," Loretta declared. "I can feel it."

"What's this about a Student-of-the-Year election, Loretta?" I asked, trying to change the subject.

"Something you'll never have to worry about, Hershell Cobwell," Loretta replied sarcastically.

"You have some very interesting friends, son," Dad said.

"We tried to be polite and entertain them while you were doing whatever it was you were doing with those other people," Mom said. "Are they your friends, too?"

My heart was in my mouth. "Uh, yes."

"Well, it's not polite to leave some of your friends alone after you've invited them over to your house so you can visit with other friends," Dad said. "You should visit with your friends all together. And if you can't do that, then you shouldn't invite so many people over all at one time."

"Well, actually . . ." I tried to say.

"Yes, we had to look at that girl's boring newspaper clippings while you were entertaining those other friends of yours," Mom said.

"You shouldn't invite people over to your house, Hershell, if you're not going to talk to them," Loretta said. "You've got a lot to learn about having friends!"

Mom walked over to the window and lifted the curtains. "All those kids are still in front of our house," she said. "I just wish they'd go home."

"Well, I'm tired. I'm going to bed," Dad said. "I don't care if they are planning to have a gang fight."

"This has certainly been a very unusual day," Loretta said.

I thought, you don't know the half of it, sister!

Chapter Five

I WOKE up several times during the night. This business with the tattoo was all beginning to seem like a dream to me, and I wasn't quite sure I'd be able to pull it off the way I had planned.

I stayed in bed later than usual the next morning. By the time I finally got dressed I only had enough time left to yell a hurried "good morning" and run out the door. I didn't feel like answering any questions, in case anybody had had a chance to think about everything that had happened the night before.

Albuquerque Wilson was at the bus stop when I got there. She smiled when she saw me.

"I heard about you last night, Hershell. It was all over the neighborhood. Was I ever impressed! May I see your tattoo?"

"I'd rather not take my shirt off here, Albuquerque. I'll show it to you at school sometime during the day."

"Gee, Hershell," Albuquerque pleaded, "I don't think I can wait that long."

I smiled a tired smile. "The first chance I get... at school. I promise."

"Do you mind if I sit with you when the bus arrives, Hershell?"

"Not at all, Albuquerque. Here it comes now."

The bus hissed to a stop in front of us, and we climbed aboard.

The driver was the same one who had taken me downtown yesterday. When he saw me, he grinned. "My kid told me all about what you did," he said. "You're his hero." Then he winked. "Some report, huh?"

"You don't know the half of it," I said.

Albuquerque and I walked to the back of the bus and sat down. I didn't know what to say to her. She just kept looking at me with those big brown eyes. I was kind of embarrassed. Albuquerque was nice, but she was no Patti Carroll Mason.

Finally, Albuquerque said, "You know, Hershell, I used to be impressed by your sister, Loretta, but now I know who's the really distinctive person in your family." She sighed long and deeply. "You're exciting to be around."

Albuquerque was making me very uncomfortable. "It's nothing," I said.

"Oh, but it is, Hershell, it is," Albuquerque insisted. "You're really special now."

"I suppose so."

Albuquerque continued to stare at me. I continued to stare straight ahead.

Then the bus began slowing down. I looked out the window. We were still several blocks from Jackson Elementary School, but there were already kids lining the streets and waving at the bus. The lines got deeper as we neared the school.

I stood up. Then I sat back down.

"What's the matter, Hershell?" Albuquerque asked.

"I don't know. I think I feel a little faint."

"I can imagine. This is heavy excitement."

"This is it!" the bus driver called. "Jackson Elementary School!" He was still grinning.

I stood up again. Albuquerque took my arm and leaned on me. We almost fell over.

"Maybe you'd better not lean on me so heavily," I said. "I might not be able to stand up."

We headed toward the open door of the bus.

When we reached it, we stopped. The crowd stretched from the curb to the entrance to the school. When they saw me, they cheered.

"You know what they want, don't you?" Albuquerque whispered into my ear.

I nodded. "But I'm not sure I can do it," I said weakly.

"You can do it, Hershell," Albuquerque assured me.

"Yeah, go ahead, kid!" the bus driver said. "Give 'em what they want!" He didn't seem to be in any hurry to leave today.

I slowly unbuttoned my shirt. The crowd began murmuring. With each button, the murmuring grew louder and I grew bolder. At the last button, there was near hysteria. I ripped open my shirt and the crowd went wild.

I knew then that everything would be all right.

Albuquerque and I stepped into the crowd.

Behind us, the door to the bus hissed closed and the driver slowly pulled away from the curb.

For a few seconds I was afraid that we would be trampled to death, but then a very strange thing happened. The crowd opened up and made a path for me and Albuquerque. We began walking toward the entrance to Jackson Elementary School.

"Wave to everybody," Albuquerque whispered into my ear.

I began waving. Everybody waved back.

When we finally reached the steps to the school, we turned and waved again. The crowd cheered. Then I rebuttoned my shirt and Albuquerque and I went inside.

"First thing I need to do," I said to Albuquerque, "is go to the principal's office and get a class pass for missing school yesterday. I don't know how I'll explain this to Mrs. Wilson."

"I'm sure you'll think of something, Hershell." Albuquerque squeezed my hand. "I have to go now, but let's ride home on the bus together after school, all right?"

"All right."

I watched Albuquerque as she headed into the crowded hallway. Then I started toward the principal's office. Everybody smiled at me as I walked down the long hall.

I tried not to act nervous, but I couldn't help it. What was Mrs. Wilson going to say about my tattoo? And would she even let me back into my classes?

I thought I'd never reach the door to her office. It seemed to get farther and farther away as I walked toward it.

Finally, I reached it and opened the door. Mrs. Wilson herself was standing behind the counter in the outer office.

I gulped.

"Yes, Hershell? What is it?" Mrs. Wilson said without a smile.

"I need a class pass, Mrs. Wilson. I was absent yesterday."

Mrs. Wilson consulted a list on the counter in front of her. "Yes, your name is here." She looked up at me. "Why were you absent, Hershell?"

The moment of truth had arrived. "Uh, well, you see, I went to the foot of Broadway yesterday, and I, uh, well, I got a tattoo on my chest."

Mrs. Wilson took a deep breath and then let it out. "I shall never cease to be amazed at what parents will let their children do," she said. Then she took her pen and wrote out a pass for me. "You may go on to class, Hershell." She handed me a pink slip of paper. "Just show this to all of your teachers."

"Yes, ma'am."

I couldn't believe Mrs. Wilson actually thought my parents had let me get a tattoo on my chest, but at least now she wouldn't be calling them to tell on me.

For a minute, I even thought about opening my shirt and showing it to her. If she could see how nice it looked, then maybe she wouldn't think it was so terrible.

But the only thing I did was shrug and back out of the office.

I backed out into a crowd of people, but the crowd parted for me. It parted all the way to Miss Wren's science class.

All the other students in the class were seated when I entered.

Miss Wren was writing on the blackboard at the

front of the room, so I walked up to her and showed her my class pass.

She nodded, then went back to writing on the board.

The other students stood up and applauded.

Patti Carroll Mason escorted me to my lab position.

Then everybody sat down.

Miss Wren turned to face the class and said, "Today, we shall be dissecting *Rana pipiens*."

"Is she that new girl from Los Angeles?" somebody asked.

The rest of the class started giggling. It sounded like a perfectly normal question to me.

I turned around. Everybody was looking at a boy who was wearing an overcoat and dark glasses.

"*Rana pipiens*, Jason," Miss Wren said without a smile, "is the common grass frog, also known as the tailless anuran."

Jason, I thought. Could this be the Jason La Chazze whose picture didn't appear in last year's yearbook, either? I had never paid any attention to him before, but there was something about him that reminded me of Elisabeth. I'd have to talk to him and find out for sure.

Miss Wren opened her mouth to continue talking about *Rana pipiens*, but she was interrupted by Mrs. Wilson's voice coming out over the public address system: "YOUR ATTENTION, PLEASE! HARRISON PESCARA, THE PRESIDENT OF THE JACKSON ELEMENTARY SCHOOL STUDENT COUNCIL, HAS AN EXTREMELY IMPORTANT ANNOUNCEMENT TO MAKE. HERE'S HARRISON!"

The loudspeaker screeched.

Then Harrison came on. "GOOD MORNING, FELLOW STUDENTS OF JACKSON ELEMENTARY SCHOOL," he began. "DURING LUNCH PERIOD, YOU WILL BE ALLOWED TO VOTE FOR STUDENT-OF-THE-YEAR. THE CANDIDATES ARE MILLICENT ADAMS, SLOANE LEE, WEBSTER COLLINS, AND MAXWELL HAVERFORD BROWN. PLEASE EXERCISE YOUR RIGHT TO VOTE. THANK YOU."

The loudspeaker screeched again and then went dead.

For the next few minutes, everybody in the class talked about whom they were going to vote for. Several times, some of the students looked over at me and grinned, but I knew they couldn't vote for me, because my name wasn't on the ballot. I was going to vote for Maxwell Haverford Brown, because his was the only name I recognized.

Finally, Miss Wren told us to get with a lab partner and she would give us some dead frogs to dissect.

Nobody had permanent lab partners. Usually, we just worked with whomever we wanted to. I usually worked with whoever was left when all the popular partners were taken. Today, I had wanted to work with this Jason, so I could find out if he was really Jason La Chazze, but before I could get over to where he was sitting, I was surrounded by Patti Carroll Mason and several other people.

"We want to dissect our frogs with you," they all said.

So what else could I do but oblige them?

Actually, it turned out to be a nightmare. I

ended up surrounded by ten totally dismembered and almost unrecognizable frogs.

When the bell rang, I had hoped to talk to Jason before he left class, but when I looked around, he had already disappeared. Maybe I could catch up with him in the hall, I thought.

But I got so busy cleaning up frog guts I was almost late for English.

Thank goodness English class was a little better than science class had been.

"We're going to write an original poem," Mr. Corvin announced.

Several people said they were going to write "Ode to Hershell Cobwell."

I wrote "On Being Distinctive." I decided that I had already had enough experience to draw upon that I could write a pretty decent poem about it.

When we finished, Mr. Corvin asked somebody to volunteer to read his or her poem. Everybody volunteered me.

When I read it out loud, though, I thought it sounded terrible, but I got a standing ovation. Even Mr. Corvin raved about how original it was.

In music class, everybody wanted to hear me sing a song, so with Mrs. Swaim accompanying me on the piano, I sang "On Top of Old Smokey." Naturally, I was a big hit.

I couldn't believe it. I couldn't do anything wrong.

Finally, it was time for lunch.

The bell rang and everybody cleared a path for me as I headed toward the cafeteria.

Then I remembered that we were supposed to vote for Student-of-the-Year during lunch period.

Well, I thought, I'll eat and then I'll vote for my good friend Maxwell Haverford Brown.

When I got to the cafeteria, there were already several kids in line ahead of me, but they all gave me cuts, so it didn't take me very long to get my tray.

I had just started to take a bite of my hamburger, when Patti Carroll Mason rushed up and sat down beside me. "I voted for you, Hershell," she said.

"For me? For *what*?"

"Oh, Hershell, don't be such a ninny. For Student-of-the-Year, of course."

"But my name isn't even on the ballot, Patti. How could you vote for me?"

"I wrote your name in, Hershell! Haven't you ever heard of a write-in candidate?"

"Uh, well, I . . ." I couldn't think of an intelligent answer. But as it turned out, I didn't have to.

Hal Hall, Terri Sue Wainwright, Spunky Madison, and Elisabeth La Chazze all rushed up to my table and sat down.

"We voted for you, Hershell," they said.

"Really?" I couldn't believe this. "Do you think I have a chance of winning?"

"Things are going really well," Terri Sue said. "I've never seen everyone here at Jackson Elementary School so excited about an election before. According to the latest tabulations I've heard, there is a ninety-nine percent turnout. It's the greatest Student-of-the-Year election in our school's history!"

"And it's all because of you, Hershell," Elisabeth added. "I've heard several people say they wrote your name in on the ballot!"

I smiled at the news.

"Well, I've got to get something to eat," Patti said. "All this excitement has made me hungry!"

"Us, too," everyone else said.

They all stood up and hurried over to the line.

I looked down at my hamburger and shriveled-up French fries. They didn't look very appetizing. I hate cold hamburgers and French fries.

"Hi, Hershell."

I looked up into the face of the Jason from Miss Wren's class.

"Hi," I said. "Is your name Jason La Chazze?"

"Yes, but . . . how would somebody as famous as you know my name? I'm nobody important . . . yet."

"Well, actually, we have a lot in common, Jason."

"Really? What?"

"Famous sisters, for one thing."

"Well, one of these days, I'm going to be even more famous than Elisabeth."

"I'm counting on the same thing with my sister, Loretta," I said.

"You haven't even touched your hamburger, Hershell. What's the matter? Wasn't it very good?"

"It's cold and I don't like cold hamburgers."

"I don't, either," Jason said. "Would you like to share my lunch? My mother always puts in too much for me, anyway."

"Uh, well, yeah, thanks. What do you have?"

"Peanut butter and jelly."

"My favorite! Here. Sit down."

Jason pulled out a chair and sat down. Then he took out his peanut butter and jelly sandwich and gave me half. He also had some apple slices and shared those with me, too.

"This is great," I said. "Do you always bring your lunch?"

"Not always. It just depends on what we're having."

We ate in silence for a few more minutes, then I said, "I thought what you said about *Rana pipiens* in Miss Wren's class was funny." I didn't admit that I hadn't understood it at first.

"Thanks. Being a comedian in class is part of my plan to become distinctive," Jason said. "That's also why I wear this overcoat and dark glasses. It sort of makes me stand out."

"I know all about trying to be distinctive," I said.

"Yeah. You've come up with a great gimmick, too. I don't know why I didn't think of that. This is something that could get a person elected Student-of-the-Year. By the way, I wrote in your name on the ballot."

"I appreciate that, Jason," I said. But he was also telling me something I really didn't want to hear. People weren't voting for Hershell Cobwell for Student-of-the-Year. They were voting for Hershell Cobwell's *tattoo*. All of a sudden it was kind of unsettling, and I didn't know what to do about it.

"I was just wondering, Jason," I said. "I've been at this school for almost seven years. Why hasn't anybody paid attention to me before?"

"You weren't distinctive before. Now you're distinctive."

"Really, Jason? But I'm still Hershell Cobwell, the same old Hershell Cobwell I was before."

"Oh, no, you're not!" Jason exclaimed. "You're

Hershell Cobwell *with a tattoo*!"

"But underneath that tattoo," I countered, "it really is the same old Hershell Cobwell."

"Don't dwell on it, Hershell. Just enjoy everything that's happening to you."

I shrugged.

Suddenly the door to the cafeteria burst open and Harrison Pescara rushed in and up to the table where Jason and I were sitting.

"We're adjourning to the auditorium," Harrison announced. "By the time everyone gets there, we'll probably have the ballots counted for the Student-of-the-Year election. I can't say anything more about it, Hershell, but I think you need to be there."

I stood up and started to follow Harrison. "Come on, Jason!" I called. "Let's go!"

Jason grinned and started after me.

Students were streaming toward the auditorium, and there were scattered rounds of applause as we passed them.

When we finally arrived, Harrison told me to sit in the front row. Jason sat down next to me.

Then Harrison led the candidates for Student-of-the-Year onto the stage. I didn't recognize any of them except Maxwell.

I could hardly contain my excitement. Even though I wasn't up on stage, Harrison must have wanted me to sit in the front row for a reason. I knew that several people had written in my name on the ballot, but that still left most of the rest of the school. How had they voted? I wondered.

Then Harrison stepped up to the microphone.

"Do we have the results of the election yet?" he asked.

Mrs. Wilson began walking down the center aisle. She had a sheet of computer printout in her hand. When she reached the stage, she handed it to Harrison.

Harrison looked at it and smiled. Then he looked at the audience.

Waves of murmurs swept across the auditorium.

"I am pleased to announce," Harrison began, "that the Student-of-the-Year is a write-in candidate . . . HERSHELL COBWELL!"

The auditorium erupted into thunderous applause.

I wasn't quite sure what I was supposed to do, so I just sat there grinning.

Then Jason said, "Go up on stage, Hershell!"

I stood up and began walking slowly toward the stage.

Harrison stepped back to the microphone. "Let the ceremony begin!" he shouted.

Patti, Debbi, Lori, Juli, Terri, and Cindi began cartwheeling down the center aisle.

When they arrived in the front of the auditorium, they formed a straight line and began to cheer. "GIMME AN 'H'!" they yelled.

The crowd yelled, "H!"

"Gimme an 'E'!"

"E!"

"Gimme an 'R'!"

"R!"

"Gimme an 'S'!"

"S!"

"Gimme an 'E'!"

Good grief, I thought, they're misspelling my name!

"E!" the crowd shouted.

"Gimme an 'L'!"

"L!"

"Gimme another 'L'!"

"L!"

"HERSHELL! HERSHELL! HERSHELL! YEA!"

The crowd stood up and applauded and stomped their feet and began chanting, "WE WANT HERSHELL! WE WANT HERSHELL! WE WANT HERSHELL!"

I stood in the center of the stage, taking it all in.

I couldn't believe that I, Hershell Cobwell, had actually been elected Student-of-the-Year. It was still a thrill, even if it really was because of my tattoo and not because of me. Just wait until Loretta hears about this! I thought.

Suddenly the crowd's chant changed to "TAKE OFF YOUR SHIRT! TAKE OFF YOUR SHIRT! TAKE OFF YOUR SHIRT!"

So I unbuttoned my shirt and took it off. I stood there under the spotlight, my tattoo in full view of everyone.

The crowd was going wild.

Then I felt somebody touch my shoulder.

It was Harrison. "Put your shirt back on, Hershell," he said. He sounded a little irritated. "We have to be going. As Student-of-the-Year, you have a lot of obligations to take care of."

"You mean I can't just go home after school and watch some television?"

Harrison looked startled. "You most certainly may not! In fact, you may never be able to go home again!"

Chapter Six

"THERE you are, Hershell!"

I looked up. Elisabeth La Chazze was standing by the doors to the auditorium. Her hands were on her hips.

I waved. "What's up?"

She started walking toward me. But I had never seen anybody walk like that before—except in the movies. What'd they call that, anyway? Oh, yeah! *Slinking!* Elisabeth La Chazze was *slinking* toward me.

Finally, she reached me. "Where have you been, darling?" she asked in a deep, breathy voice. "I waited for you after the Student-of-the-Year ceremony, but you just disappeared."

Darling? Did she call me *darling*? I gulped. "Uh, Harrison Pescara had some things he wanted to discuss with me."

"Well, you're finally here, darling, so that's all that matters."

"Listen, Elisabeth, if you're not feeling well, I . . ."

But Elisabeth stopped me with, "What makes you think I'm not feeling well, darling?"

"You're talking kind of funny, that's why."

Elisabeth made a face. "I was talking like Tallulah Bankhead, Hershell!" she said in her normal voice.

"Who's Tallulah Bankhead?"

"A great stage actress." Elisabeth shook her head in disbelief. "Don't tell me you've never heard of Tallulah Bankhead."

I shrugged my shoulders. "Sorry, Elisabeth."

"Never mind. It's all right." She gave me a smile. "Come on. We need to start rehearsing for the All-School Play." Elisabeth grabbed me by the arm and we headed toward the doors to the auditorium.

"Are you sure this is a good idea, Elisabeth? I've never been in a play before."

"Yes, of course, I'm sure. I told Lydia I wanted you to have a very important role this year."

"Who's Lydia?"

"Lydia Putnam. The other music teacher, Hershell." Elisabeth looked at me as though I had been living on another planet. "She takes all of my suggestions when it comes to serious drama."

"You mean you call Ms. Putnam *Lydia*?"

"Yes, Hershell. Theater people are like that. We're all very close."

"Oh," was all I was able to say.

"This year, for a change, the All-School Play will be a serious drama with romantic overtones," Elisabeth continued, as we entered the auditorium.

"I thought it was always a musical, where all the little kids dressed up like flowers and things like that, and the sixth graders talked about them."

Elisabeth shook her head. "It always has been, but I told Lydia that I thought we should do something different this year. Naturally, she agreed."

"I still can't believe that you want me to be in it. Do you really think I'm good enough?"

"Of course, I do, Hershell. In fact, I want you to be my love interest."

I stopped walking down the aisle. "Did you say *love* interest?"

Elisabeth looked at me and a strange expression came to her face. She closed her eyes and puckered her lips. "Yes, Hershell," she said in that deep, breathy voice again.

My stomach was beginning to feel very funny. "What do I have to do?"

Elisabeth opened her eyes. "You have to kiss me on the mouth!"

"On the mouth?" I cried. "I can't kiss you on the mouth! I'm . . . I'm just not ready to kiss a . . . girl!"

Elisabeth stamped her foot, hard. "Hershell, the role calls for it!"

I was beginning to sweat.

Elisabeth grabbed me by the arm and almost dragged me the rest of the way down the aisle and up the steps that led to the stage.

There was a sofa just out of view of the auditorium. Elisabeth pulled me over to it and we both sat down.

"I thought we could practice just a little before Lydia gets here," Elisabeth whispered. "I want you to be perfect in this part."

I was getting short of breath.

My shirt was sticking to my back.

We were now close enough that I could smell Elisabeth's sickly sweet perfume. It wasn't helping my stomach at all.

"Open your shirt so I can see your tattoo, Hershell, and then kiss me," Elisabeth said in her deep, breathy voice.

What was I going to do? I looked around frantically.

Then the door to the auditorium opened, and I heard somebody coming down the aisle.

I jumped up.

"Hershell! What's the matter?" Elisabeth cried.

"Somebody's coming. They'll see us!" I whispered.

"Is that you, Elisabeth?" It was Ms. Putnam.

Elisabeth took a big breath and let it out. It was obvious she was disgusted. "Yes, it's me, Lydia! Hershell Cobwell's here, too." she called. "I wanted to see how well he could handle the kissing scene."

I almost lost my stomach again. There was no way to get out of this now. I'd be the laughingstock of the school. I'd be distinctive all right! But not in a way I wanted to be!

Ms. Putnam came up onto the stage. "Hello, Hershell," she said. "I'm delighted that Elisabeth wants you to be in the All-School play."

"Thank you, but I don't know if I can handle the kissing scene or not."

"Oh, there's nothing to it," Ms. Putnam said. "On cue, you simply take Elisabeth's hand, raise it to your lips, and kiss it. It's simple."

"What about on the mouth?" I asked.

Ms. Putnam looked at me and grinned. "Why, Hershell, you sly puss, you. I would never have figured you for that sort of thing."

I felt myself getting redder and redder.

"No, I'm afraid that in an elementary school

play, we'd better leave off kissing on the mouth," Ms. Putnam continued. "We might upset some parents."

I looked over at Elisabeth. She was giving me a funny grin. It scared me to death. I could tell that she wasn't going to give up.

I couldn't believe the predicament I was in. How was I going to stay popular and not have to kiss Elisabeth La Chazze in the All-School Play?

For the next thirty minutes, Ms. Putnam had me read my lines. First with my shirt buttoned. Then with my shirt open so she could see the tattoo. I even kissed Elisabeth on the hand a couple of times.

"The tattoo reading is definitely better," Ms. Putnam said finally.

"I think so, too," Elisabeth said. She started to put her hand on my chest. But I turned and began buttoning my shirt.

"That's all for today," Ms. Putnam said.

"I think Hershell and I should stay around and practice," Elisabeth said hurriedly.

"That might be a good idea," Ms. Putnam agreed.

"No!" I cried. Elisabeth and Ms. Putnam looked at me strangely. "I mean, no, I think I have go someplace else. I have other student leaders I need to visit."

I hurried off the stage.

Now I was in big trouble! Not only did I have to worry about kissing Elisabeth La Chazze on the mouth, but Ms. Putnam wanted me to keep my shirt open during the play. What if my parents came? They'd see my tattoo. Of course, maybe I could tell them it was just makeup. I'd have to think about this some more.

Being popular was really turning out to be an incredible strain.

When I left the auditorium, I stopped and leaned up against the hall wall for a minute.

Harrison Pescara rushed up to me. "What's wrong? Why aren't you visiting with some of the student leaders? It's expected of you, Hershell. After all, you are Student-of-the-Year!"

"I am, Harrison . . . or at least I *was*. I'm just about to go find somebody else to talk to."

"Well, hurry up. You can't waste time. You need to be on your way."

"I was just catching my breath, Harrison." I didn't feel like explaining that it was because I was running away from Elisabeth La Chazze so I wouldn't have to kiss her on the mouth.

Harrison laughed. "Popular people never have time to catch their breath. As Student-of-the-Year, you are now popular." Then he turned and rushed off down the hall.

I didn't know where to go next. I knew it was my duty as Student-of-the-Year to get to know all the different groups of kids at Jackson Elementary School, but . . .

Suddenly, I heard the sound of motorcycles coming from the end of the hall, so I decided to check it out. I started walking.

I followed the sound until I reached the Vocational Workshop. This was where sixth graders who weren't in the band or didn't play sports built wooden things and learned how to take apart metal things. Most of the punks hung out here.

I opened the door. Seated on the floor around a cassette tape player were Hal Hall and the rest of the sixth-grade punks.

"Hey, man!" Hal said when he saw me. "Come on in! We've been waiting for you. Sit down!"

I looked at the floor. There were grease spots all over it. "Where do you want me to sit?"

"Right here," Hal said. He pointed to one of the bigger grease spots. "You're lucky, man. We saved the biggest spot for you."

I sat down. I could feel the grease soaking into my jeans and through my underwear. I was very uncomfortable.

"Let me start the tape over," Hal said. "I want Hershell to hear all of it."

"Yeah, man," the rest of the punks said.

"Tape?" I asked.

"Yeah, Mr. Lacombe lets us listen to motorcycle tapes during class, so we'll know what we'll be taking apart when we get to high school vocational classes," Hal explained. "It's great."

"Oh." I looked over toward Mr. Lacombe's desk. He had his feet up on his desk and was reading a newspaper.

Hal rewound the tape. "The first sound you hear is that of a Suzuki GV700G1 Madura." Then he started the tape.

"Louder!" shouted one of the punks sitting at the back of the room.

Hal turned up the volume. It was deafening.

"Man, ain't that great?" Hal said.

"Yeah, it is," I shouted. But I was wondering if being popular meant you had to go deaf.

The room was vibrating from the sound of the motorcycle tape.

"Now, that's a Moto Guzzi 850-T5," Hal shouted, as the tape continued to play.

"Oh?" I couldn't tell any difference.

I was afraid that I wouldn't be able to hear *anything* ever again if he didn't turn down the volume.

Hal suddenly stopped the tape. "Now, when I start this tape again, we're going to hear the Cagiva WMX-250, the Kawasaki KX250, and the Yamaha YZ250."

All the punks cheered.

Hal turned the tape back on. It still all sounded the same to me. Loud!

When Hal finally turned the tape off, everybody ran to a table at the end of the room.

"What do we do now?" I asked. "Build something out of wood?"

"Now we read magazines," Hal replied. "See that stack of magazines over there? That's all the cycle magazines from the last ten years. Mr. Lacombe saves them all for us."

"Does anybody ever *ride* a motorcycle around here?"

"Not yet. We ain't old enough. But sometimes Mr. Lacombe gets some of the high school kids to bring theirs to class, and we all take turns sitting on them. Of course, we have an old one of our own that Mr. Lacombe bought for the class. We take it apart and put it back together during class sometimes."

"Sounds like a lot of fun."

"It is."

I sat down next to Hal and read through several

magazines. That lasted about an hour. I was beginning to get hungry. "Well, are we planning to do anything else today?"

Hal looked at his watch. "We need to get dressed." He blew a whistle.

Everybody stood up and began putting on their leather caps and leather jackets.

Hal looked at me. "You'll need to buy an outfit. You can't cruise the malls with us in clothes like that."

"Where can I get one?"

"There's a place near the foot of Broadway that sells the best leather outfits in town. I'll take you there this weekend."

"Okay."

Everybody was now dressed and standing in a line. Hal took a can of oil off a shelf, stuck his hand in it, and then started wiping oil all over his clothes. Then he handed the can to me.

"What am I supposed to do with it?" I asked.

"Follow my example," Hal said.

"Uh, is there a reason for this?"

"Well, the only way we can get greasy is to do it this way, since we ain't old enough to ride motorcycles. Just take a handful of oil and wipe it all over your shirt and pants."

I stuck my hand in the can and began wiping the oil all over my shirt and pants. Mom was going to die.

Then I passed the can to the next person in line. He grinned at me. He looked like he had already put some oil on his teeth.

When everybody had finished wiping oil all over

themselves, Hal took a can of dirt and mixed some of the oil with it.

"What's that for?" I asked.

"You can't have clean fingernails if you're going to be a punk," Hal said.

When he finished mixing the oil and the dirt together, he stuck his hands in it, dug them around for a couple of minutes, then took them out and held them up for us to see.

His fingernails were all black.

"Man, ain't that beautiful! They've never been this dirty before!"

Then Hal handed the mixture to me. I did exactly as he had done. Then I held my hands up for everybody to see.

There was applause. "Filthy!" everybody shouted.

Then I passed the mixture to the next person in line.

Finally, after everyone was prepared, we began to leave.

"See you Saturday," Hal called to me, "and we'll get you some punk clothes."

But one of the other punks ran up to Hal and whispered something just as I started out of the room.

"Hey, Hershell, wait a minute!" Hal shouted to me.

I stopped. "Yeah?"

Hal's eyes were on my chest. "Us punks would like to see your tattoo. You know, up close and personal like."

"Sure thing." I began opening my shirt. Murmurs of excitement passed through the punks.

When my tattoo appeared, a loud cheer went up.

Tears came to Hal's eyes. "You make us all proud to be punks, Hershell."

"Thanks, Hal," I said. Then I left.

The first place I headed was the rest room to wash all the dirt and grease off my hands and to get as much of it off my clothes as I could.

Harrison Pescara was just coming out. "I've been looking all over for you, Hershell. A lot of the student leaders have been wondering where you were. You're not getting off to a very good start as Student-of-the-Year, are you, and I'm afraid . . ."

"Listen, Harrison," I interrupted, "I just can't go anywhere else today. I'm tired and I'm hungry and frankly, I'm a mess."

Harrison looked at me with disgust. "You should have visited with the punks last."

"Now you tell me."

"You'll learn the ropes, Hershell. It just takes time. But you've got to remember that a Student-of-the-Year is a popular person, and popular people have no time of their own. Their time belongs to others. You'll have to give up some of the things you've been used to doing."

"Yeah, like eating and sleeping."

Harrison smiled. "We eat too much and we sleep too much. Popularity has its price."

"This is just my first day as Student-of-the-Year, Harrison. Can't I wait until tomorrow to be more popular?"

"If that's the way you feel about it, Hershell. But just remember that a lot of very important and *popular* people worked very hard to put you where you are today. You owe us!"

"I don't mind being popular, Harrison, it's just that . . ." I tried to say.

But Harrison said, "Well, Hershell, if you get an early start tomorrow morning, then maybe you can get all of your visits in. I'll try to smooth things over with the rest of the student leaders."

"Thanks, Harrison."

"I'm not saying I'll be able to, though. I'm just saying that I'll *try*."

"I'll appreciate anything you can do," I said.

But Harrison had already disappeared down the hall.

Chapter Seven

WHEN I opened the door to our house, Mom, Dad, and Loretta were sitting on the sofa in the living room.

Mom was crying, Dad had a sad expression on his face, and Loretta just looked disgusted.

"Where have you been this time, Hershell Cobwell?" Loretta demanded. "You weren't here again this afternoon when I got home from school!"

I wanted to tell them all about my being elected Student-of-the-Year, but I knew this was neither the time nor the place. "Well, uh, I . . ."

Then the telephone started ringing.

"Don't you realize how disquieting this is for me?" Loretta continued. "I'm used to hearing that noisy television set when I get home. These last two days have been very difficult, Hershell. I don't like my schedule interrupted like this!"

"What do you mean? I haven't interrupted your schedule!"

"Oh, but you have, Hershell, you have! I open the door, I hear the television set, then I start nagging you about wasting your mind on those silly programs you watch. I haven't been able to nag you for the last two days. Nagging you is a very important part of my day, Hershell!"

"Well, I'm sorry, Loretta, but frankly, I don't give a . . ."

"You're being very inconsiderate of me, Hershell Cobwell!"

The telephone continued to ring.

"Isn't somebody going to answer that?" I said.

"Why should *we* answer it?" Loretta said sarcastically. "It'll just be for you." She looked at Mom and Dad, then back at me. "Look at the grief you have caused my parents!" she cried.

Her parents, I thought.

"Where *have* you been, Hershell?" Mom finally said through her tears. "It's just not like you not to be here when I get home from the university. I thought something terrible had happened."

"Yes, son," Dad said. "We were very worried."

"Really? I didn't think you cared."

"DIDN'T CARE?" Mom and Dad shouted. "OF COURSE WE CARE!"

"Well, that's not exactly what I meant to say, it's just that, well, you're always so busy, it's . . ." I couldn't finish the sentence. The telephone was driving me crazy.

I walked over and picked up the receiver. "Hello. Oh, sure, I've heard of you. You live in that big house with the swimming pool in the backyard and your mom and dad both drive Mercedes. Tomorrow night? Well, I guess so. Thanks. Thanks a lot. See you then."

"What was that all about?" Mom asked.

"That was Bobby Barnsdall. He's in the fifth grade. He's really rich, and he wants me to come to a party at his house tomorrow night."

Mom and Dad just looked at me.

"That telephone hasn't stopped ringing since I got home from school today," Loretta said. "Why are kids all of a sudden interested in you, Hershell Cobwell?"

"I thought you were going to find out for yourself, Loretta," I challenged her.

"Don't get smart with me, Hershell Cobwell," Loretta snapped.

"Actually, it's very simple. I'm just popular all of a sudden, that's all. People have discovered me. Yeah, that's it. People have discovered me!"

Loretta's eyes narrowed to slits. "There has to be a reason. There's a reason for everything."

"Are you hungry, son?" Dad asked. "I think there's some chicken left."

I was glad that Dad had changed the subject. "Yeah, I'm real hungry."

The telephone started ringing again.

"I think we should take the receiver off the hook!" Loretta shouted.

"I agree," Mom said with a sob.

"We can't," Dad said. "I'm expecting a very important call from the office. I can't miss it!"

I picked up the receiver again. "Hello." My stomach was beginning to churn. "Tomorrow? Well, I'm already invited to a party over at Bobby Barnsdall's, so . . . well, I'd hate for you to change the date just for me, but . . . yeah, I'm not doing anything day after tomorrow. Are you sure you won't mind calling all those other people to tell them about the change? What if they can't come then? Oh? Well, I've never been to a birthday party where I'm the only guest, but thanks for inviting me." I hung up the receiver.

"My life is topsy-turvy," Loretta said, "and I don't like it one bit!" She glared at me. "My grades are beginning to fall. I missed a math problem today. I never miss math problems."

"And I'm finding it difficult to grade papers," Mom said. "I've never had trouble before. I couldn't grade *anything* last night."

"Your dinner is in the oven, Hershell," Dad said. "It's probably all dried up by now."

I went into the kitchen and took my food out of the oven. I could hardly tell what it was.

The telephone started ringing again, but I decided to let it ring and concentrate on trying to figure out what I should eat of my dinner and what I shouldn't.

I had just decided not to eat the black part, when Loretta finally answered the telephone.

"HELLO!" she screamed into the receiver. "JUST A MINUTE! HERSHELL! IT'S FOR YOU, AS IF YOU DIDN'T KNOW!" To Mom and Dad, she added, "MY NERVES ARE ABSOLUTELY SHOT!"

I picked up the extension in the kitchen. "Hello. No, I can't tonight. I'm tired. Tomorrow night? No, sorry, I'm busy. I'll be over at Bobby Barnsdall's. Actually, I'm busy for the next three nights, but after that . . . Okay, I'll be there. Thanks for asking me." I hung up the receiver.

Loretta had come into the kitchen and was eyeing me carefully. "What could be so interesting about you now that you're being invited to parties all of a sudden?" she said.

"Nothing," I said hurriedly.

"I know that, but obviously nobody else does. I'm going to get to the bottom of this yet."

"You keep saying that, Loretta, but you don't do anything about it."

"Don't you worry, Hershell Cobwell," Loretta said through clenched teeth. "I'll find out!"

And deep down, I knew she would find out, too, or at least die trying, but I still said, "Don't bother me now, Loretta. I'm tired and I'm hungry. It isn't easy being as popular as I am!"

"*You're* tired and hungry!" Loretta screamed again. "What about me? What about Mom and Dad? *Our personalities are changing because of you!*"

I decided not to pursue this conversation any further, so I did what I always do to force Loretta to leave the room when I'm eating. I started smacking.

"You're disgusting, Hershell Cobwell!"

"That's not what all my new friends think."

Loretta stalked off without saying anything else.

For the next two hours, nobody said a word. Mom, Dad, and Loretta all just looked at me with strange, frightened eyes. They couldn't understand what was happening to me . . . *or to them.*

I began to get very nervous again.

There were a lot of times when I would walk around the house without a shirt on. I knew I couldn't do that anymore. How long would it be before they realized and asked me why?

Or when would one of my friends slip up and mention the tattoo in front of them before I had had a chance to explain?

I simply had to come to grips with my problem and figure out a way to tell them that wouldn't put my life in danger.

If I had only known that being distinctive would put so much stress on me, I might have reconsidered getting the tattoo in the first place.

But there was no way I could return it. I had it for life!

The telephone continued to ring off the wall. All the calls were for me. Within an hour, I had been invited to a party every night of the week for the next month.

Dad was getting upset because his important call hadn't been able to get through.

Finally, I took the receiver off the hook of the telephone in the living room, where I didn't think Dad would see it.

"The telephone hasn't rung for an hour," he muttered to me once when he passed me in the kitchen. "I wonder why I haven't received my call?"

I didn't say anything, but I had begun to feel kind of sorry for him and Mom. Incredibly, I had even begun to feel a little sorry for Loretta.

Finally, around ten o'clock, they all sat down together in the kitchen. Mom and Dad had a cup of tea, and Loretta had a glass of warm milk.

"I'm going to bed," I said. What I didn't add was that I couldn't stand being around them anymore.

But nobody paid any attention to me. They just continued to stare into space.

I went upstairs, took my shower, put on my pajamas, and then got into bed.

Then I got out of bed, took off my pajama top, and looked at my tattoo in the mirror. It was a little red around the edges. I hadn't noticed that earlier. But it kind of set off the rose and the lettering of "MOTHER" nicely.

When I touched it, though, it felt a little warm and a little sore. I guessed that was probably normal.

I continued to stare at it.

Less than forty-eight hours before, I had stood in this very room, looking at myself in front of this very mirror—a nobody. Now I had been elected Student-of-the-Year and commanded the attention of everybody at Jackson Elementary School.

Instead of going to bed, I should be up making plans for my future, I thought.

But I suddenly began to feel warm all over, so I put my pajama top back on, got into bed, and turned out the light.

That was when a rock hit my window.

I jumped out of bed and looked out. There was a crowd of girls in our front yard. I opened the window to tell them to go home when another rock came flying up. I had to duck to keep from getting hit.

"What do you want?" I called out. But I tried not to do it so loudly that my parents and Loretta would hear me.

"We want to see it!" one of the girls yelled up.

"Oh, good grief," I muttered. "Oh, all right!" I shouted. "But be quiet! Besides, it's so dark, you won't be able to see anything."

"Oh, yes, we will," said another one of the girls. "We brought an industrial strength flashlight with us!" Then she produced the biggest flashlight I had ever seen.

I had just opened my pajama top to reveal my tattoo when I was blinded. I covered my eyes. I thought I could actually feel the heat of the flashlight on my skin. It made me feel even warmer than I already felt.

Below me, the girls had begun to scream.

"If you don't be quiet," I shouted down to them, "I'm going to put my pajama top back on!"

But the screaming was so loud that they couldn't hear me.

"Hershell?" It was Dad in the hallway outside my room.

I hurriedly shut the window and pulled the shade. "Yes, sir?"

"What's going on in there?"

"Nothing."

Outside, the screaming was getting louder.

"Are you sure?" Dad asked.

"I'm sure, Dad." It wasn't really a lie. If you got technical, there wasn't anything going on *inside* my room.

"It's probably just those new people across the street," Dad continued. I didn't know whom he was talking about. "Ever since they moved in, they've had nothing but rock music parties. This neighborhood just hasn't been the same."

"Yeah, that's probably it. Well, good night."

"Good night, son."

I could hear him muttering to himself as he walked back down the hall.

I went back to the window and pulled up the shade. The screaming, if anything, had gotten even louder.

I opened the window.

"WE WANT HERSHELL! WE WANT HERSHELL! WE WANT HERSHELL!" They had begun to chant. I was sure that the crowd had gotten larger, too.

When they saw me at the window again, they turned the flashlight back on.

"Turn that off!" I shouted, "and I'll come down!"

A cheer went up and the flashlight went off.

I thought about it for a minute. I couldn't go downstairs and outside. Somebody might see me. I could, however, climb out through the window.

The branches of the big mulberry tree in front of our house brushed against my window, so I reached out, grabbed a branch, and swung onto the top of it.

The cheers below were deafening.

Once I had steadied myself, I started climbing down. I hadn't done this in years. I used to do it all the time.

I tried to remember *exactly* how I used to do it, when I was still a little kid, a couple of years ago, and slowly, it began to come back to me.

I held on to one branch, swung over to another, then started feeling my way down.

All of a sudden, it was like the old days, and it felt good.

I descended the tree slowly. Below me, the screams had intensified.

I looked down once and saw that a crowd of girls had completely circled the trunk of the tree and were reaching up to grab me.

But I continued climbing down.

Finally, I reached the lowest limb. Then I

stopped. "You'll have to move, so I can swing down," I shouted.

The crowd parted. I sat down on the branch, grasped it with both hands, then swung down, and landed on my feet.

It stung for a few seconds. Then I looked around. I had never before been in the middle of a crowd of screaming girls. I didn't know what to say.

I was trying to think of something when it happened.

Actually, it seemed to happen slowly, just like one of those slow-motion movies.

One girl reached out and grabbed my pajama top and tugged at it. I pulled loose.

Then another girl behind me began tugging at it. That started it.

Before I could do anything about it, I was being jostled back and forth. I heard my pajama top rip, and then it fell off me.

That's really how I was saved.

While the girls were on the ground, scrambling for my pajama top, tearing at each other to get a piece of it, I jumped to a branch, pulled myself up, and was halfway up the tree before anyone realized what had happened.

I thought that was the end of it. I'd just climb up the way I had climbed down and then go back to bed.

But somebody suggested climbing up the tree after me. Three girls took up the challenge.

I was beginning to feel like a dog being chased by cats.

I began climbing as fast as I could.

I finally reached the top branches. The only

thing that could save me now was to get through my bedroom window and lock it.

Then I noticed that it was closed. I had forgotten to put a stick under it to keep it open. It had fallen shut.

I held on to a branch with one hand while I tried to open the window with the other. But it was stuck. It did that sometimes. But why did this have to be one of those times?

I looked down. One of the three girls was nearing the center branches of the tree. She had a maniacal grin on her face that scared me to death. This was all like a very bad dream. I didn't know what I was going to do.

I leaned over and tried to open the window again. But it wouldn't budge.

The girls were getting closer, especially the grinning one. I'd have to use my foot as a weapon to fend them off.

Just then sirens sounded and lights flashed and a police car arrived—all in the nick of time, too.

The girls on the ground cleared a path for it.

"Where's the kid who's stuck up in the tree?" one of the policemen shouted.

"Here I am!" I screamed.

The policemen turned their spotlight on me. I began waving frantically.

The girl with the maniacal grin stopped grinning and gave me a dirty look.

The policemen shooed the three girls out of the tree and one of the officers began climbing up to where I was.

When the policeman reached me, I said, "How did you know I was up here?"

"Your neighbors across the street called," he replied. "They said the noise was disturbing their rock party. How'd you get up here, anyway?"

"It's a long story."

"Well, come on, let's go down."

"Uh, wait a minute. Could you just help me open this window? It's my bedroom window, and if I could just go back to bed, it would certainly save me a lot of explaining."

The policeman was looking at my chest. "Say, you're that kid with the tattoo, aren't you? My kids have been telling me all about you."

"That's right. So do you think you can help me get this window open or what?"

"Sure, anything, I'll be glad to help. You're my kids' hero."

"I'll send you an autograph."

"Hey, man, would you really?" The policeman continued to look at my chest.

"The window?" I prodded. "Do you mind?"

"Oh, yeah, sure." He reached over and pushed on it and it came up.

Then he helped me climb back inside.

"Don't forget the autograph," he said.

"I won't," I promised.

Then I watched him as he climbed back down the tree.

The crowd was beginning to disperse. When the policeman reached the ground, I closed the window and pulled the shade.

Then there was a knock on my door.

Oh, no, I thought. This is it! Loretta and my parents know everything. The game's up. "Yes?"

"May I come in?" It was just Dad. He didn't

sound angry, either. Maybe, just maybe, my secret was still safe.

I started toward the door.

Then I remembered that I didn't have my pajama top on. Dad would see my tattoo! I grabbed a shirt off the chair just as he came into my room.

"Well, that party across the street has finally quieted down," he said. "Couldn't you sleep either?"

He doesn't suspect anything, I thought. I breathed a sigh of relief. "It was rather difficult, wasn't it?"

Dad looked at me for a moment. I hadn't seen him look at me that way in a long time. "Hershell, son," he said gently, "if there's anything bothering you, I'd like for you to tell me about it. I'll try to be understanding."

"There's nothing bothering me, Dad, honest. Everything's just great. I've never been happier in my life."

Dad sighed and said, "Well, all right."

I smiled at him. "Good night, Dad."

"Good night, Hershell."

After he had left, I went back to the window and peeked out the shade. There were a few people still milling around outside. They looked up at my window from time to time.

In the glow of the streetlight, I could see what was left of my tattered and torn pajama top, evidence that I had just barely survived another day of being distinctive.

Chapter Eight

I KNEW something was seriously wrong when I woke up the next morning. I was hot all over. My chest felt like it was on fire.

I got out of bed, walked weakly to the mirror, and looked at myself.

My face was red.

I slowly took off the shirt that I had slept in. That was when I got the shock of my life.

My tattoo was all red and bumpy. The rose looked wilted and "MOTHER" looked misspelled.

And furthermore, I felt awful. So I went back to bed.

But I knew I couldn't stay there. If I stayed home, then somebody would telephone the doctor, and everything would be up!

No, I had to get back out of bed and get ready for school.

I stood up again. I felt even weaker than before.

I took another look in the mirror at my tattoo. It really looked terrible. What had Harry said about infection, about it happening to one in a million and that I wasn't even close to the magic number? Well, ha, ha, Harry, I thought, I certainly fooled you. I'm it. What was I going to do?

Getting dressed was one of the hardest things I have ever done. It hurt me to move. But I had to get dressed and get out of the house to think.

I finally got my shirt on. Then I sat down on the bed and slowly pulled on my pants.

But I knew my socks and shoes would take more effort.

I started my panting exercises . . . ah, ah, ah, ah, ah, ah, ah, ah, ah, ah . . . and got my socks on. I did my shoes the same way. Finally, I tied my laces and stood up.

Then I opened my bedroom door slowly and slipped down the hall to the bathroom. I went inside and locked the door. Somehow I managed to wash my face and comb my hair and brush my teeth. It was a major experience with pain.

Then I went back to my room, got my books, and started quietly down the steps.

"Hershell, is that you?" Dad called.

"Yes."

"Breakfast is ready, son, and I don't want you leaving until you've eaten something."

"But Dad, I have to be at school early to make up a test I made a bad grade on," I lied.

"Oh, well, okay, son."

I try never to lie, really, but when I need to, that's always a good excuse. For one thing, it's very believable. Everybody in my family believes that it would be very easy for me to have made a bad grade on a test and, having done so, besmirched the good Cobwell name. I am never challenged.

"Yes, yes, you must certainly do that, Hershell!" Mom called out.

"I should say so, Hershell!" Loretta shouted.

I reached the front door and was outside before anybody could say anything else.

I had hoped that by leaving early I could also miss seeing Albuquerque, but she was at the bus stop, waiting for me.

She smiled.

I tried to smile back, but I only grimaced. I'd have to work on that. I couldn't give away to *anybody* that something was desperately wrong with me.

"I didn't want to miss riding the bus with you, Hershell," Albuquerque said. "I've been here since seven A.M."

I frowned.

"Is there anything wrong, Hershell?"

"Oh, no, no, no," I said hurriedly. I felt the pain lines increasing in my face. "Why would you think there was anything wrong?"

"Well, for one thing, your face is bright red, and for another, you just sort of look like you're in a lot of pain."

"I didn't sleep too well last night."

"I know how you feel. There sure was a lot of noise in the neighborhood last night, wasn't there? Did you hear all that screaming and all those sirens? I looked out my bedroom window once and even saw a huge beam of light. It looked like it was coming from the direction of your house."

But before I had to attempt an explanation, the bus arrived. Thank heavens, there was a new driver today.

Albuquerque followed me to the back of the bus. Oh, for the good old days when all she wanted to do was read her social studies book.

I was beginning to ache all over. I didn't think I was going to make it.

I groaned all the way to Jackson Elementary School. Albuquerque kept looking at me with concern.

Since we were early, there wasn't a crowd waiting in front of the school for my arrival. I didn't think I could have stood it if there had been.

Albuquerque helped me off the bus and up to the front of the building.

"I'm worried about you, Hershell. I think you might have the flu."

That's it, I thought, the flu! "You're probably right, Albuquerque. I'm glad you reminded me of that possibility."

"You should have stayed home, Hershell. I think I ought to call your parents."

"No, no, don't do that!" I almost screamed. I tried to calm down. "You see, my parents really did want me to stay home today, Albuquerque, but there are so many things I have to do, you know, as Student-of-the-Year."

"You're such a success, Hershell. That's because you don't think of yourself first. I think it's wonderful that you're willing to sacrifice your health for the betterment of the students at Jackson Elementary School."

I grimaced.

"Are you in pain?" Albuquerque asked again.

"I'm afraid I am."

"Well, at least you can go see the school nurse."

"NO! I mean, no, I don't want to bother her. I'll just suffer."

"You're so strong, Hershell. I'll help you to your

first class if you want me to."

"I'd like that very much, Albuquerque." I leaned on Albuquerque's shoulder and we started walking down the hall.

Miss Wren was already in the classroom, washing the test tubes, when Albuquerque and I walked in.

"Hershell, is there anything wrong?" Miss Wren asked. "You look absolutely red!"

"Nothing, nothing," I managed to say. "I'm just a little tired, that's all. I didn't get much sleep last night."

"There were all sorts of strange things going on in our neighborhood last night," Albuquerque said. "There were sirens and screaming and beams of light and . . ."

"Well, don't you think you should go back home, Hershell?" Miss Wren said. "You may have the flu."

"That's exactly what I said, too," Albuquerque said.

"No, I'll be all right," I said weakly. "I just need . . . to rest . . . a . . . little."

Miss Wren gave me a concerned look, then she said, "Well, all right." Then she went back to washing test tubes.

"I really hate to leave you, Hershell," Albuquerque said.

"I'll be all right. I'll just study my science book until it's time for class."

"If you need anything, I'll be in Miss Gordon's English class. Just have Miss Wren call me on the P.A. system, and I'll come running."

"You're too kind, Albuquerque."

Albuquerque smiled. “I’m a lucky girl, knowing you as intimately as I do.” Then she backed out of the room.

After Albuquerque left, I decided to put my head down on my desk for a few minutes.

Patti Carroll Mason shook me awake. Miss Wren was talking about hydrochloric acid.

I couldn’t believe that I was feeling even worse than before.

“You look absolutely awful,” Patti whispered. “Are you sick?”

“No, no, I’m fine,” I groaned.

But I wasn’t fine. And I was getting less fine all the time. I raised my hand.

“Yes, Hershell?” Miss Wren said.

“I think I need a drink of water. My throat feels kind of funny.”

“All right, Hershell, but I’m sending you to the school nurse, too.”

I started to protest, but I didn’t have the strength. I had never been to the school nurse before, so I really didn’t know what to expect. I’d just have to play it by ear.

Miss Wren wrote out a pass and brought it back to my desk. “You poor dear,” she said.

Everybody in the class was looking at me now. I had the funniest feeling that they all knew exactly what was wrong.

I could hardly stand up. But I finally did and was able to shuffle out of the room.

Behind me, the students had started whispering. Pretty soon, it would be all over school that something was wrong with Hershell Cobwell!

I stopped at the water fountain and drank and

drank and drank. Then I started shuffling down the hall toward the nurse's station.

"HALT!" somebody called out behind me in a military-sounding voice.

I turned slowly. It was Collin Cutty, the school hall monitor for this period.

"Oh, I didn't know it was you, Hershell." Collin's eyes were glued to my chest. "But I'll have to see your tat . . . er, I mean, your hall pass, anyway."

I handed it to him.

Collin checked off something on the clipboard he was carrying. "Not feeling well?"

"It's probably just the flu."

"There's a lot of that going around."

I didn't say anything.

"Well, I've got to go up on the second floor," Collin finally said. "You wouldn't believe how many people try to leave their classrooms without hall passes. It's my job to see that they don't."

Collin turned and started toward the stairs. I could tell that he enjoyed his work immensely.

I continued shuffling toward the nurse's station. When I finally reached it, I collapsed against the door.

It was painful even to turn the knob.

When I finally got the door open, the nurse looked up at me from her desk. It was obvious that she recognized me. She probably could hardly wait to tell me to take my shirt off. This whole thing would be over in just a few minutes. But I almost didn't care.

"Just have a seat, Hershell," the nurse said with a smile. "I'll be with you in a minute."

Then I noticed that somebody else was lying on

the cot. It was Jason La Chazze.

"What's wrong with you, Jason?" I asked.

"I think I may have the flu," Jason replied weakly. "What's wrong with you?"

I looked at the nurse. "Uh, I think I may have the flu, too," I said.

"There's a lot of it going around now," Jason said. Then he closed his eyes.

I moved Jason's overcoat and dark glasses aside and sat down on the red plastic couch.

I was beginning to sweat. I didn't know if it was because I had a fever or because I was scared to death. When this all came out, I'd be the laughingstock of Jackson Elementary School.

My parents would disown me, too. This would be the last straw. They'd say, "You've besmirched the Cobwell name for too many years, and it has to stop. You may no longer use the Cobwell name. You'll just have to use whatever name the family who adopts you has." Then of course Loretta would add, ". . . if you're lucky enough to find somebody who wants to adopt you!"

I was feeling faint. I had to get out of there. I stood up slowly.

Then I remembered Jason's overcoat and dark glasses on the couch and it gave me an idea. I looked at the nurse. She was writing something on a chart.

"Be with you in a minute, Hershell," she said without looking up. "You might as well go ahead and take off your shirt."

I let out a gasp.

The nurse stood up and went into another room.

I looked at Jason. His eyes were still closed.

"Jason, I've got this big problem," I whispered, "and I need to borrow your overcoat and dark glasses."

Jason half opened his eyes. "Well, sure, Hershell, go ahead." Then he closed his eyes again.

I picked up his overcoat and put it on. Then I put on his dark glasses. Now, nobody would recognize me until I could decide what to do.

Then I slipped quietly out of the nurse's station and into the hall.

Nobody was around. I headed for the exit. I had no idea where I was going, but I knew I couldn't stay here any longer.

"Hershell!"

I turned around. Harrison Pescara was just coming out of the restroom.

"Hershell! Is that you?" Harrison shouted.

"No!" I shouted in a loud whisper.

Harrison looked at me strangely.

"I mean, yes!" I said.

Harrison started walking toward me. What was I going to do now? I could turn and run. Yes, that's what I could do. But what would that get me? So I just stayed where I was.

Harrison reached me and said, "Why are you wearing Jason La Chazze's overcoat and dark glasses?"

I looked down. "Oh, I must have picked them up by mistake. I thought they were mine." I took off the glasses and the coat.

"You look positively red, Hershell. Are you sick?"

"More than you'll ever know," I muttered.

"I'm sorry, Hershell, I didn't hear you."

"More than you'll ever know," I managed to say a little louder.

"That sounds rather cryptic. Is there something that you'd like to discuss with me?"

I looked at him for a minute. I guessed if I couldn't trust Harrison, then whom could I trust? He'd been very helpful yesterday, when I'd been named Student-of-the-Year. "Harrison, there is something. It's something very serious."

Harrison nodded toward the restroom. "We can talk in there."

I followed Harrison into the restroom.

Harrison leaned against a sink. "What's wrong, Hershell?"

"Well, Harrison, it's just that . . ." Then I stopped and bowed my head.

"You can tell me, Hershell. I'm your friend, and it's my job to help you get used to being Student-of-the-Year. I want to do whatever is necessary." He smiled. His brilliantly white teeth sparkled.

"Oh, I knew you'd understand, Harrison. I knew I could count on you."

"Of course." Harrison smiled again. "Just tell me what the problem is."

"I can do better than that, Harrison. I can *show* you."

Harrison blinked. "Well, uh, okay."

I slowly began unbuttoning my shirt. It made my skin ache whenever the cloth touched it. But I finally got it unbuttoned. Then I slowly pulled it open. Now, I thought, here's somebody who can help me decide what to do.

Harrison's eyes got wider and wider. He inhaled

slowly, then he shouted, "That's disgusting, Hershell Cobwell!"

"I can't help it, Harrison. My tattoo is infected."

Harrison's eyes got even wider. "You're... you're... you're a PHONY!" he screamed. Then he ran from the rest room, shouting "HERSHELL COBWELL IS A PHONY! HERSHELL COBWELL IS A PHONY! HERSHELL COBWELL IS A PHONY!"

I was stunned. I didn't know what to do.

I looked around. Could I hide forever in one of the stalls? I wondered.

The sweat was pouring off my face, but I felt very cold.

I put Jason's overcoat back on. Then I looked at myself in the mirror. I didn't like what I saw, so I put Jason's dark glasses back on, too.

Then I slowly opened the door to the restroom and stuck my head outside.

Harrison was running down the hall, shouting into every classroom, "HERSHELL COBWELL IS A PHONY! HERSHELL COBWELL IS A PHONY! HERSHELL COBWELL IS A PHONY!"

I closed the door slowly and leaned up against it. What I wanted to do now was cry.

But what I did was walk over and splash some cold water on my face.

I looked at myself in the mirror again. Where could I go now? I wondered. I certainly couldn't go back to class. I couldn't go home, either.

Then it hit me. I could go see Harry at his tattoo parlor. He'd know what to do.

I opened the door again. There was nobody around. They were all probably in their classrooms, voting to name a new Student-of-the-Year.

I stepped out the door and started down the hall toward the exit.

"HERSHELL!"

I turned and saw Lori, Juli, Cindi, Debbi, Terri, and Patti. They were lined up across the hall, giving me the evil eye.

Then Patti snapped her fingers and they all started running toward me.

I started running toward the door.

If they caught me, there was no telling what they'd do to me!

I made it to the exit just in time and pushed through the glass doors.

A city bus was pulling up to the bus stop in front of the school.

Fear gave me the strength to continue running.

"Wait up!" I shouted. "I have to get out of here!"

Chapter Nine

As SOON as I got on the bus, I collapsed onto the front seat.

"It's a dollar, kid," the driver said.

I looked up. "Huh?"

The driver was the same one who had taken me to the foot of Broadway when I got my tattoo, but he didn't seem particularly friendly today. He probably didn't recognize me wearing Jason's overcoat and dark glasses. It was just as well. I didn't feel like explaining anything to him.

"It costs a dollar to ride the bus," he repeated.

If there was one thing I knew, it was that I didn't have any money on me today. "Uh, well, let's see."

"I'm not pulling away from the curb until I get a dollar from you."

What was I going to do now? I wondered.

Then it occurred to me to look in Jason's overcoat pockets. I found $2.25 in small change.

I stood up slowly, braced myself against one of the poles, and deposited one dollar in dimes.

The driver gave me a dirty look and lurched away from the curb so fast that I almost fell.

There were only three other passengers on the bus, but they all gave me dirty looks, too.

I had used what little strength I must have had in reserve just running across the school grounds to catch the bus. I was absolutely sapped. It was all I could do just to shuffle down the aisle to the rear.

I finally made it to the back seat and sat down by a window.

Now I was hot, so I took off Jason's overcoat, but I decided to leave on the dark glasses.

Then I got cold again, so I put the overcoat back on.

I kept putting the overcoat on and taking it off. One of the passengers who was sitting just a few seats in front of me kept turning around to look.

I could tell I was making her nervous, but I couldn't help it. One minute I was hot, the next minute I was cold.

The closer we got to downtown, the more people got on the bus.

Finally, a man sat down next to me. He was one of the biggest men I had ever seen. When it came time for me to take the overcoat off again, I couldn't, because he was sitting on it.

He looked so mean that I didn't want to ask him to move, so I just sweated. Finally, I got cold again, so it didn't make any difference.

The bus finally arrived at the foot of Broadway. I didn't have to ask the big man to get off the overcoat, because he was getting off the bus, too.

By the time I shuffled to the door, the driver was about to start off again.

"Wait a minute!" I shouted.

The driver looked in the rearview mirror and scowled.

But I didn't care.

Just as my foot touched the sidewalk, the bus roared away from the curb.

I began walking slowly toward the Deep Blue Sea Locker Club.

When I arrived, I went in and headed straight for Painless Harry's Tattoo Parlour. Harry was working on a sailor, who was sound asleep. There wasn't anybody else around.

"Harry!" I whispered.

Harry was so engrossed in the eagle he was tattooing on the sailor's chest that he didn't notice me.

"Harry!" I said a little louder.

Harry looked up. "I'll be finished in a minute, fellow." He seemed irritated. "You're not supposed to interrupt an artiste at work."

"This is important, Harry," I persisted. I took off my dark glasses. "Do you remember me?"

Harry looked at me for a minute. "Listen, I get a lot of people in here, you know, because I have this here reputation for the finest tattoos in town. Should I know you?"

I took off Jason's overcoat and hung it on a chair. Then I stood facing Harry. "Yes, you should."

"Are you all right, sailor?" Harry asked slowly.

I slowly unbuttoned my shirt and pulled it apart.

Harry's mouth dropped open. He looked down at the sailor in the chair to make sure he was still out, then he whispered sharply, "Not here!"

He grabbed me by the arm and hustled me into

a back room. There was a dim light hanging from the ceiling.

"Well, do you remember me *now?*" I asked.

"Yeah, yeah, I remember you. What happened?"

"Well, I'm the one in a million, Harry."

"Huh?"

"You told me that only one in a million tattoos gets infected. I guess I'm that one."

"Oh, great. Just my luck. Well, what do you want *me* to do about it?"

"It hurts, Harry. Don't you have any medicine or something that I could take to make it better?"

"Look, sailor, I'm not a doctor, okay? So why come to me? What about the Navy? They'll take care of you."

"Well, it's sort of like this, Harry, I'm not in the Navy. I'm in the sixth grade and . . ."

"What?" Harry screamed. "You said you were in the Navy!"

"No, I didn't. I didn't say anything. You just assumed I was in the Navy."

"Well, why didn't you tell me you weren't?" Harry demanded.

I shrugged my shoulders. "I just sort of liked the idea."

"Oh, great. This is all I need." Harry looked at me. "Have you told your parents yet?"

"No. In fact, they don't even know I have a tattoo. I was saving it for a big surprise."

"Good. Save it a little longer."

"But everybody at school knows. In fact, right now, they're probably voting on another Student-of-the-Year to take my place."

Harry looked puzzled.

"I need help, Harry," I pleaded. "I can't go home. My parents would disown me."

Harry ran his fingers through his greasy hair. "Let me think, kid. Just let me think."

"Hey! Where are you?" the sailor shouted from out front.

Harry stuck his head through the curtain. "Just a minute. I needed to get some more ink. Go on back to sleep."

"Okay!" the sailor said.

Harry was beginning to sweat. "Uh, listen, kid, there's a free clinic just a few blocks from here. They don't ask no questions, see? Go over there. They'll take care of you."

"A couple of blocks from here?"

"Yeah, yeah, it's on Hayes. Just go out the main entrance, turn left up Johnson, then you'll hit Hayes. The free clinic's on the corner."

"I think I've got it."

Harry looked at me with pleading eyes. "Don't mention my name. Okay? They might close me down."

"Don't worry, Harry. All I want is to get well."

"Listen, I'll tell you what I'll do. I'll give you back the ten dollars that tattoo cost you. How about that?"

"It cost me fifteen, Harry, and I gave you a dollar tip, too."

"Oh, yeah, that's right."

I started to walk out into the main parlor.

"Wait a minute!" Harry hissed. "Button up your shirt first. I don't want anybody to see that. They might get the wrong idea."

I buttoned up my shirt, then I followed Harry back out front.

I put on Jason's overcoat and his dark glasses.

Harry went to the cash register and took out sixteen dollars and handed it to me.

"Thanks, Harry," I said.

But he only turned and started working on the sailor again.

I left the Deep Blue Sea Locker Club and headed for the free clinic.

A block from the free clinic, the street turned mean-looking and I thought about stopping, but my chest was hurting so much that I couldn't. Actually, Jason's overcoat and dark glasses helped me fit right in with the people on the street, so I went on.

When I got to the free clinic, I was shocked. I didn't know what to expect, but it wasn't anything like Dr. Abercrombie's Clinic in the San Diego Medical Square, just a few miles from our house. It wasn't anything like San Diego General Hospital, either. This place was a boarded-up building that had "Free Clinic" painted over where the words "Fried Chicken" had been before.

It took all of my courage just to open the front door. In fact, what made me do it was another look at my tattoo. It was all puffy and yucky-looking.

When I opened the door, an awful smell came out, but I held my breath and went inside.

The waiting room was crowded with people of all colors.

There was a woman sitting at a desk near a rear

door. She smiled when she saw me. I walked up to her.

"My name is Her . . . uh, Jason La Chazze." It was the only other name I could think of to say.

"You don't have to give me your name, son. All I need to know is what's wrong with you."

I looked around. Nobody in the room was paying any attention to me. They all looked sad and sick.

I looked back at the lady. "My tattoo's infected," I whispered.

She blinked. That was probably a new one on her. She started to write down something on a clipboard, but then she looked up at me again. "How old are you?"

"I'm eleven," I whispered.

I could tell that she wanted to say something like, "Does your mother know about this?" But she had probably been trained not to ask questions other than the ones that were absolutely necessary.

"It really hurts," I said, after she had finished writing down some things on her clipboard.

She smiled again. "Well, I think Dr. Dickerson can take care of you, but you'll have to wait your turn."

"I don't have much money."

"It doesn't cost anything. That's why it's called a *free* clinic."

"Oh, yeah, I forgot." I looked around, then turned back to her. "Do I just sit down or what?"

"Anywhere you can find a seat. You're number fifteen. I'll call you when it's your turn."

I found a seat near her desk. I didn't want her to forget me.

The person sitting on one side of me was asleep. The other person was reading a torn magazine.

After a few minutes, the person who had been sleeping woke up just in time to hear his number called out. It was like he knew just how long to sleep.

One by one the other people were called in, but nobody ever came out. I was getting kind of nervous.

"What's happening to all the people who go inside?" I asked the woman reading the magazine. "They never come out again."

"Your first time here?" she asked.

"Yeah."

She kept looking at me.

"I just got into town," I added. "I'm from New York."

"Oh, yeah, well, ain't that interesting? I'm from Hollywood myself. I'm between pictures."

"Really? I've never met a movie star before."

She rolled her eyes. "After you finish with the doctor, you go to the pharmacy to get some medicine, then you go out another door. What's wrong with you, anyway?"

"My tattoo's infected."

"Sure, kid," she said, then she picked up her magazine again and started reading.

Finally my number was called and I went through the door. A nurse pointed me into a small room that sort of looked like where I go when I see Dr. Abercrombie.

I took off Jason's overcoat and sat down on a chair.

"You're eleven years old and your tattoo's infected?" the nurse said.

"That's correct." I was beginning to feel embarrassed, but the nurse didn't act as though anything was strange.

She took my temperature and blood pressure and checked my pulse, then wrote down something on her clipboard. "Take off your shirt, please," she said finally.

I slowly unbuttoned my shirt and took it off.

"It does look bad."

"It really hurts."

"I believe you." The nurse wrote down something else on the clipboard. "Dr. Dickerson will be here in a minute," she added. Then she left.

I was all alone with my throbbing tattoo.

I looked around the room. I was glad that I had come. The doctor would look at the tattoo, give me some medicine to make it better, then let me out the back door, and that would be that.

But then what was I going to do? I couldn't go home. I couldn't go to school. No way. Maybe after I left here I could go to one of those shelters that give you something to eat and a place to sleep. I'd ask this Dr. Dickerson if he had any addresses.

I bet they'd give me work at the shelter, too, so I could earn enough money to buy a bus ticket up to Los Angeles. They probably had bigger shelters up there, where you could stay as long as you wanted to.

The door opened and a black man wearing a white coat came into the room. He had a clipboard in his hand. "Good afternoon, I'm Dr. Dickerson," he said.

"Good afternoon, I'm . . . uh, Jason La Chazze."

Dr. Dickerson looked at me for a minute. Then he looked down at the clipboard. Then he looked back at me. "You're eleven years old and your tattoo's infected?"

"That's correct."

"Well, let's take a look at it, then."

Dr. Dickerson examined the tattoo for several minutes. Then he examined the rest of me.

Then he said, "Where are you from?"

"I live here in San Diego, at 5534 Hillcrest Drive."

"That's a nice part of town."

"It's all right, I guess."

Dr. Dickerson looked at me again for a couple of minutes, then he put down his clipboard. "Normally, I don't ask my patients too many questions, but I'll have to admit that I don't get too many eleven-year-old boys with infected tattoos, either. Would you care to tell me about it?"

"Sure, why not? It all started when I wanted to be distinctive." Then I told him the whole story.

After I finished, he said, "And you really don't think you can go home or back to school again?"

"Are you kidding me? I'm a failure. I can't do anything right. The kids at school would laugh at me. My parents would disown me. And my sister Loretta, well, there's no telling what she would do! No, I thought maybe you could give me the addresses of some quality shelters for the homeless where I could stay for a while until I got back on my feet. Then I could earn enough money to ride the bus up to Los Angeles, where . . ."

"I can give you some medicine to kill the infection in the tattoo," Dr. Dickerson interrupted, "but I will not give you the addresses of any *quality* shelters for the homeless. I am, however, going to give you some advice."

"What's that?"

"Go home!"

"I told you I can't do that."

"Why not?"

"Because I'm not distinctive anymore, that's why. Haven't you been listening to me?"

"Oh, but you *are* distinctive, son."

"Yeah, I'm the only eleven-year-old kid in San Diego with an infected tattoo. In fact, right before I left school today, this guy I thought I could trust was running from classroom to classroom telling everybody that I was a phony."

"But you've learned that to some people what's on the outside is the only thing that matters, not what's on the inside, right? Well, very few people realize that, so that makes you distinctive, doesn't it?"

I just looked at him. What I didn't need now was a simple explanation of what had happened to me.

Dr. Dickerson smiled. "I've just examined your insides and they're perfect. It's what's on the outside, this tattoo, that's causing you the problem. We can take care of that easily. I'll give you some medicine, like I said." He paused. "If you had had problems on the inside, well, then that would have taken a lot more work."

I didn't want to admit that some of this was

beginning to make sense. I let out a big sigh. "I suppose you're right."

"Of course I am," Dr. Dickerson said. He smiled again. Then he handed me a cup of water and a large pill. "Swallow this." Then he wrote down something on a pad of paper. "Take this to the pharmacy down the hall and be sure to follow the directions on the label."

I stood up. "Thanks," I said.

"Good luck," Dr. Dickerson said. Then he opened the door for me and I started down the hall.

Chapter Ten

BUT back on the street, Dr. Dickerson's advice didn't seem so hot after all. I started to go back and ask him if he could give me those shelter addresses just in case, but the door I had just come out of didn't have an outside knob. I'd have to go back through the front entrance, and I knew I'd never get in to see him again just for that, so I kept on walking.

I felt better the closer I got to Broadway.

When I got to the bus stop near the Deep Blue Sea Locker Club, there was a bus that I could have taken to my house, but I didn't.

I just leaned up against a building and let the buses come and go.

The sun had almost set when I decided that I'd better do something. New people were arriving on the street and they looked even worse than the ones who had been there during the day.

I got on the next bus that would take me home.

Of course, I thought, I didn't have to go straight to my house when I got there.

I sat at the back of the bus and looked out the window. I was still getting hot and cold, but for some reason, I really was beginning to feel better.

We passed Jackson Elementary School and finally arrived at my bus stop.

I got off the bus and just sat on the bench for a few minutes, trying to decide what to do. There was nobody around that I recognized. I was glad. I didn't think that I could stand to see any of my *former* friends.

Finally, I stood up and started walking.

First, I walked slowly. Then I started to think honestly about what Dr. Dickerson had said, and I began to pick up speed.

I didn't have to be Student-of-the-Year to be happy. I could just be me, and if somebody wanted to be my friend, he could, and if he didn't want to, then he didn't have to.

I was beginning to get hot again, so I took off Jason's overcoat.

Then it hit me! That was it! I'd have to return Jason's overcoat and dark glasses sooner or later. I bet he'd still be my friend. He wouldn't care if I had an infected tattoo.

Of course if I became good friends with Jason, I'd have to think up a way of dealing with Elisabeth. I couldn't stand the thought of her trying to kiss me on the mouth from now on! But I figured Elisabeth probably wouldn't want to be friends with me anymore, either.

I smiled and started walking faster.

I'd tell Mom and Dad and Loretta all about my tattoo. I'd come clean. I'd start all over. I wouldn't keep secrets from them. My life would be an open book. My friend Jason La Chazze and I could . . .

I had reached my house.

This wasn't going to be so hard after all, I

thought. But I had trouble opening the front door, because my sweaty hands kept slipping on the knob.

Finally I got it open and went inside.

Loretta and Mom were sitting in the living room. They looked up when I came through the door.

"Hershell, where have you been?" Mom said. "They telephoned from your school today. They said you left in the middle of the morning. It was a very strange conversation."

"Yes, Hershell," Loretta said. "Where have you been?"

"I'll explain everything in a minute. First I need to talk to Dad."

"He's upstairs, taking a shower," Mom said, "but you know he doesn't like to be disturbed when he's taking a shower."

"This can't wait!" I shouted, and I started running up the stairs.

"Hershell!" Mom shouted. "Wait until your father is dressed before you try to talk to him!"

"It's all right, Mom!" I shouted back. "I've already studied that stuff in school!"

"Hershell!" Mom almost screamed.

The bathroom was steamy but empty, so Dad had to be in his bedroom. The door was closed.

All families have the same rule, I guess. Stay out of your parents' bedroom if the door's closed. But this was too important to wait.

I grabbed the knob and turned it and burst into the bedroom.

Dad was standing in the middle of the room. All

he had on was his boxer shorts. He looked stunned when he saw me.

"Hershell!" he cried.

Then he grabbed a shirt off the bed and covered his chest.

But not before I had seen it.

On his chest was a tattoo: a single rose, with "MOTHER" written across it. The funny thing was that the rose looked wilted and "MOTHER" looked misspelled.

I couldn't believe it. I had never been so happy in my entire life. I knew now that everything was going to be all right.

Dad was just staring at me. Finally, he said, "Well, what is it that you want, Hershell?" He didn't sound too happy.

I started unbuttoning my shirt. "I have something to show you, Dad," I replied.